T0150396

WHICH WAY?

←→

THEODORA BENSON

First published in 1931

This edition published in 2021 by
The British Library
96 Euston Road
London NW1 2DB

Cataloguing in Publication Data
A catalogue record for this publication is available from the British Library

ISBN 978 0 7123 5398 4
e-ISBN 978 0 7123 6713 4

Text design and typesetting by JCS Publishing Services Ltd
Printed in England by CPI Group (UK), Croydon, CR0 4YY

CONTENTS

⬅ ➡

The 1930s	v
Theodora Benson	vii
Preface	ix
Publisher's Note	xi

PART I
The Four Cross Roads — 1

PART II
Approaching the Cross Roads — 5

PART III
Turning to the Left — 53

PART IV
Going Straight On — 97

PART V
Turning to the Right — 143

PART VI
Which Way? — 195

Afterword — 199

The 1930s

→ **1930:** 769,239 babies are born in the UK – a 30 per cent decline from 1900. Throughout the rest of the 30s, the number stays below 750,000, before rising again in the 1940s.

→ **1930:** 2,635 women receive university degrees in UK – 29 per cent of the total awarded. This percentage had dropped by the end of the decade and wouldn't rise above a third until the 1980s.

→ Marie Stopes' influential work *Married Love*, published in 1918, has sold 750,000 copies by 1931. While relatively conservative, it explains sex and sexuality frankly and means that far fewer women start marriage ignorant of what consummation entails.

→ The 1930s is the decade where films with sound, commonly known as 'talkies', overtook silent films. The transition is not immediate; the first talkie is released in 1927, and silent films continue to be made throughout the 1930s, but the 'silent era' is widely considered to be over.

→ **1931:** There are 3,764 divorces in the UK.

→ **1931:** *Which Way?* is published.

→ **1931 (October):** Ramsay MacDonald remains Prime Minister in a landslide general election victory for the newly formed National Government.

➥ Book-of-the-month clubs become very popular in this decade, where readers receive monthly books chosen by a panel of noted authors and critics. Intellectuals are often disparaging of them, but tens of thousands of readers subscribe to their lists, receiving novels by authors such as Virginia Woolf and D.H. Lawrence, as well as more 'middlebrow' works.

THEODORA BENSON
(1906-1968)

Theodora Benson was born Eleanor Theodora Roby Benson in 1906, the third child of Dorothea and Godfrey Rathbone Benson, later Lady Charnwood and 1st Baron Charnwood – at which point their daughter became The Honourable Theodora Benson. The family lived at Stowe House in Lichfield, Staffordshire, and both Benson's parents were writers: her mother wrote books about her collections of autographs and manuscripts, as well as three novels, and her father was a biographer specialising in American presidents.

Benson's first novel, *Salad Days*, was published in 1928. It was critically and commercially successful, and Benson followed with several novels in quick succession. When *Which Way?* appeared three years later, it was her fourth novel. Benson's writing has been described as 'presenting a cynical world of failed romance, lost ideals, social foibles and ruthless self-seeking', while *Which Way?* has been singled out as particularly experimental.

Alongside her prolific novel output, Benson also co-wrote several irreverent books with her childhood friend Betty Askwith, including *Muddling Through, or Britain in a Nutshell* which opens, 'Sense of humour is a very exclusive quality. Only the English have it.' She also turned her hand to mystery writing, horror short stories, and travel writing – visiting most of the countries in northern Europe, often with Askwith, as well as several countries in Asia.

During the Second World War, Benson published *Sweethearts and Wives: Their Part in War*, a short book illustrated with photographs from the home front, designed to encourage women to take up war work in support of soldiers. She also worked as a speechwriter for the Ministry of Information, where the novelist and biographer Elizabeth Jenkins was her assistant.

Benson never married, which Jenkins attributed to the youthful failure of a romance with a man whom her mother considered unsuitable. On Christmas Day 1968, Benson died of pneumonia while staying with her sister, at the age of 62.

Preface

How would my life have turned out if I'd made a different choice? It's something we all probably think about at times. In this extraordinary novel, Theodora Benson allows the reader to play out three different versions of the heroine Claudia's life, each the consequence of the seemingly trivial decision of where she should spend a weekend away. At the start of each parallel narrative, Claudia comes into an empty room, with two invitations in her hand and the telephone ringing. She makes her choice, and we explore the vastly disproportionate effect that simple decision has on her relationships, her future and even her personality.

Which Way? was published in 1931. Benson was only 25 but already had a number of her novels in print. The experimental form of *Which Way?* is indicative of her growing confidence as a writer.

The idea of alternate histories had been around for a long time, but writers had usually focused on huge tipping points, such as the outcomes of wars. *Which Way?* was published in the same year as a book called *If it Had Happened Otherwise*, edited by J.C. Squire, and containing essays by Winston Churchill, Hilaire Belloc, and G.K. Chesterton, among others. Each chapter imagined the world as it would have been had an historical event turned out differently. Readers were asked to imagine the communist Britain that could have resulted from a successful General Strike of 1926. They were also presented with a Louis XIV who had avoided execution by embracing a constitutional monarchy, a decision which had ensured his survival and had the knock-on effect of preventing the American War of Independence from taking place. With great success, Benson applied the same method employed by Squires and other historians to the life choices of an average person.

Benson's friend, the author and biographer Elizabeth Jenkins, commented in Benson's obituary that her writing showed 'gracefulness, immediacy and realism, and a flair for experiment'. *Which Way?* manages to be both highly evocative of the early 1930s and to have something to say about relationships and social interactions in the twenty-first century.

Tanya Kirk
Lead Curator, Printed Heritage Collections 1601–1900
British Library

Publisher's Note

The original novels reprinted in the British Library Women Writers series were written and published in a period ranging, for the most part, from the 1910s to the 1950s. There are many elements of these stories which continue to entertain modern readers, however in some cases there are also uses of language, instances of stereotyping and some attitudes expressed by narrators or characters which may not be endorsed by the publishing standards of today. We acknowledge therefore that some elements in the stories selected for reprinting may continue to make uncomfortable reading for some of our audience. With this series, British Library Publishing aims to offer a new readership a chance to read some of the rare books of the British Library's collections in an affordable paperback format, to enjoy their merits and to look back into the world of the twentieth century as portrayed by their writers. It is not possible to separate these stories from the history of their writing and as such the following novel is presented as it was originally published with minor edits only, made for consistency of style and sense. We welcome feedback from our readers, which can be sent to the following address:

British Library Publishing
The British Library
96 Euston Road
London, NW1 2DB
United Kingdom

PART 1

THE FOUR CROSS ROADS

> There was a young man who said: "God!
> Does it not seem to you very odd
> That that walnut-tree
> Should continue to be
> When there's no one about in the quad?"

There was no one in the room. Blinds and curtains were closed; the light of the skies, if any, was shut out. There was about the place the curious, expectant air of a stage set for the curtain to rise. For while hill and plain and valley are eternal and care not what fugitive dramas take them for setting, a room exists only for men and women. It is there to hear their many lies and their frightened truths; to shelter their secret thoughts; to look on at their moods of helpless revolt—things can never be the same again. … I must do something! … I must do something! … And there is nothing to do but have a bath and go to bed. An empty room is always waiting.

There was a fire in the room; very comforting and gay. It threw a lovely liquid sheet of orange on the big armchairs each side of it. It sent a flickering glow on to the gallery table where lay weekly and daily papers, magazines, a few books lately thrown down. In front of the fire was a low stool, behind that a deep, soft sofa. Against one wall were shelves of books; opposite, a writing table framed by the dull, peach-coloured curtains of the windows. Branches and trails of flowers stood in great jars, drained of their colour in the shadows but not of their faint sweetness. The cushions were fluffed out, inviting. An antique clock marked time in a hushed monotone. Only the fire was alive, consuming its life—for what? Then the door opened and as Claudia came with hurried steps into the fire's glow, two open letters in her hand, the telephone began ringing. She shut the door and turned up the lights.

PART II

APPROACHING
THE CROSS ROADS

1

Nature, red in tooth and claw.
TENNYSON.

The hush and the rapture of youth in the holy places.
NOYES.

The world is too much with us.
WORDSWORTH.

When Claudia Heseltine first went to kindergarten Miss Angus, the mistress who was taking the paper mat class, put her next to a girl older than the others but backward, who tried to be kind to her. This girl, Mary, was humble and craved for affection, so Claudia, like all the rest before her, promptly repulsed her. She wanted desperately to secure similar attention from someone more popular and assured. After hanging about wistfully on the outskirts of groups she ultimately worked her way into them by dint of a campaign of trenchant snubs to other new girls, such as "don't teach your grandmother to suck eggs," or "I'll buzz my satchel in your phiz." When she had thus asserted her individuality the world began to smile upon her. The other new girls wept.

Claudia became firm friends with Cecily, a most influential girl of eight summers and some gymnastic prowess. Then there was a little boy named Jack who greatly admired her. He used to follow her about and offer her presents which she always refused. He often proposed and was roughly rejected. He was not allowed to sit next her in class, nor would she eat his sweets or use his pencils or betray her weakness for his dying pigs and clockwork mice. One day an uncle gave him a super knife, a glorious affair with every kind of instrument and blade. He pressed it on his beloved who was overcome with its magnificence and took it. Naturally she could not then help letting him sit beside her for arithmetic. Having gained this advantage the faithful Jack persecuted her with diligence, saying on every occasion:

"After all, I did give you that lovely knife."

Claudia, thus admonished, endured him, but it was not possible to find pleasure in the possession of the knife. At length, goaded and hunted, she determined to return the beastly thing and be free of him: horrors, blow, hang, dash, she had lost it. Claudia kept her money, very properly, in a china pig with a slit in his back and a trap door in his belly. She took it out, all of it, and bought a beautiful clockwork car which she gave to Jack just before prayers. He sat next her through geography and scripture in a dream of excitement and delight. During break he approached her, all elation and sudden hope. She swung her arm straight from the shoulder and slapped his face with her whole strength.

Claudia was fond of reading and devoured eagerly the charming books of fantasy that people such as Aunt Louisa gave her. The fact that she enjoyed these delightful and well-written stories as much as tales of bloodcurdling adventure or trash, together with the fact that she was an enchantingly pretty child, caused Aunt Louisa to imagine that her play must be delicious and whimsical. Whenever Aunt Louisa succeeded in overlooking it she was curiously disappointed. She would pay surprise visits to the nursery when Cecily had come to tea, and she would find the two little playmates drawing pictures of tortures in their copy books, plaiting plasticine into each other's hair or urging one the other: "Give me a twizzle, do."

Once when she came in, her niece and Cecily were reiterating angrily at each other:

"I didn't."

"You did."

"Didn't."

"Did."

"Didn't."

"Did."

"Didn't."

"Did."

She tried to produce peace and order. Cecily called out "All right! Silence in the pig market, let the old sow speak first!"

She walked into this just as she had walked into the "Say 'iced ink,' quickly" catch. She adored the children but they did not think much of her. She had a look of Mary in her yearning, prominent eyes. Among the many secret societies they had got up or joined at school was one for poisoning aunts with paint water.

Her parents were pleased with the promise of character Claudia showed. They hoped she would continue to be strong-minded and stand up for herself and know what she wanted and not drift. After all she had her softer side. She loved Cecily, and Nanny, and Mummy, and Daddy, and God. She was very good (beyond painting the soles of his feet green) to Mustard Middley, her middle-sized and mustard-coloured Teddy bear. And she was devoted to her two guinea-pigs, Startling and May.

Claudia did not continue to be so strongminded. At thirteen, when she had ceased to be enchantingly pretty and entered upon the awkward stage, the love of beauty suddenly flowered in her with such violence that she became a little mushy. The sadness of the world profaned so much beauty and sweetness and all that wonder so vast and elusive that she could not reach or hold it. She wanted everyone to be happy, good too if it could be arranged, but happy anyway. She was very austere and pure and single-hearted, very religious, rather priggish and sentimental, and sadly apt to blush and stammer.

This stage was mitigated a little by the time when, at the age of fourteen, she was so lucky as to make a great friend. This was Eileen Northover, a girl one year younger than herself. Happily they were suitable friends for each other; their parents made friends too; they came to stay at each other's houses. The two girls learnt tennis together, tried to teach themselves pole-jumping, and had an endless communion of small private jokes which caused them inordinate laughter. Happily however they did not neglect to cultivate their more serious sides. They read a lot of Swinburne and Kipling, and they wrote a bit themselves. In the kindergarten Claudia had been a poet. She had written a popular verse which ran:

> Miss Pencock teaches us plain and purl,
> She's a jolly funny old girl.
> She's got lots too many double chins,
> Hope the Kaiser'll kick her shins,

which was of course a shining example of groundless optimism. Now she conceived a really great poem which began:

"O vastness of the sea! My small soul shrinks …" But, fortunately or otherwise, it never got further.

They took much exercise, bicycling to all the villages of their two neighbourhoods and eating doughnuts, lemonade and éclairs in the principal tea shops. Claudia named her bicycle Oateater after Byron's horse at Oxford; Eileen named hers Black Beauty. Claudia, as it happened, was Sir Christopher Wren and Eileen was Our Sovereign Lord King Henry of Navarre, until the sad day when historical research revealed to her that he had had mistresses. At this discovery Eileen wept exceeding bitterly. Claudia was light-hearted about it and advanced a theory that in some vague way it was rather charming of him.

The two were sent to the same boarding school. From the first they looked eagerly forward to growing up and leaving it. They duly suffered from intense moods, from the morbid atmosphere inseparable from a large community of undiluted female young, and from feeling Very Old; but it was with horror that they at last arrived at the time when Claudia, now seventeen and the elder of the two by a year, was to leave that moderately pleasant existence to return to it no more. She went off to a finishing school in Paris and embarked on a new stage.

From Miss Eileen Northover to Miss Claudia Heseltine.

DARLING CLAUDIA,—I felt powerful gloomed yesterday thinking of you so far away among those frogs. Talking of frogs, never put French tags in your letters again, a vile affectation. What's wrong with English? And still talking of them, have you eaten any, as we Provincials do hear tell they're a dainty in your parts. Which reminds me, my breakfast egg was high. You are a sweet writing so often, but I have been pretty good, haven't I? Your letters are a light spot in a dark and earnest world. I am thinking very hard and often ask myself whether to be or not to be. You should read Boswell's *Johnson*: it's prime. It's no good talking to me about French poetry: there isn't any. Less of all this about your gewgaws and fallals: Life is real in these parts as you perfectly well know, and time was when you very properly despised all such flippancies, but now I see they are dragging you down into hell. Yesterday was Marjorie's birthday. I gave her a Swinburne, and Muriel gave her *Poems of To-day* and Joan gave her a new Life of William of Orange. Felt powerfully depressed on Sunday owing to the approach of old age and the presence of indigestion so had a good cry. Joan asked me yesterday whether God really cared. I didn't exactly know so told her I preferred to keep His secrets.

Your loving
EILEEN.

From Miss Claudia Heseltine to Miss Eileen Northover.

DARLINGEST HEART,—I love you a lot and I often come all over homesick for you. I do love your letters.

It seems funny to hear of you all giving Lives of William of Orange to Marjorie for her birthday. I am getting Jane a silk hankie and a Jack-in-the-box for hers. I'll try not to tell you about the gewgaws and fallals, but you will be just the same when you come on here: it's not that we are different but just that there is quite another atmosphere. At a finishing school there's an air of frivolity, and you let that side of you rip and conceal your love of poetry and your yearnings if any! At a pre-finishing school there's an air of morbidity, and you conceal your weakness for scent and nail polish, and your ambition to shine among the alleged *crème-de-la-crème*. (Sorry! Another French tag! My sinful linguistic pride. However, any really good dictionary will give you crème.) Really and truly, you'll find this a good spot.

Talking of spots, my back has come out in them, though fortunately a girl's face still remains quite a taking bit of work. From under the wing of Mlle. Dubois I peer out at the godless Frenchmen on the wicked boulevards, but you will be relieved to hear my morals have not gone the continental way.

Unlike school they talk a little about men here. A few speculate as to why so-and-so hasn't proposed. I have a private theory that the reason men don't propose is that they do not want to. But I hardly like to advance it.

All your own

CLAUDIA.

P.S. There are lots of jolly things in Paris but sightseeing is a hollow mockery without you. The others I only want to go shopping with—and was sorry they liked Michael Angelo's Slave as much as I did! It's a shame being parted but I do have lots of fun. Keep on missing me, my sweet.

P.S. ii. Do you think Paris will teach you to brush your hair?

After a year of that sort of thing Claudia returned home to come out and be presented. She was "finished." In a way, she was really finished. Her future alterations were not stages, they were phases. She might improve, develop, degenerate. But she was now—no matter how she might change in appearance, pose, outlook or circumstances, no matter how much knowledge the world might bring her—the complete substance of all the Claudias there could be thereafter.

2

Dis, qu'as tu fait, toi que voilà,
De ta jeunesse?

VERLAINE.

What sort of images come to a girl's mind if she wants to remember what life was like the year before last? Probably tunes come first. She fox-trotted to:

Dancing Baby, we mustn't,
Dancing Baby, be good,

and waltzed to:

You gave me a rose in the garden,
But now all my roses are blue.

Tunes generally belong to some particular young man. "Clive adored that one. How well he danced! Isn't it funny to think we were rather attracted?" Tunes have shows attached too. "Oh, didn't that come out of *This Year of Disgrace*? Then that must have been the year Daisy Jay did that superb turn about the woman golf champion. I really do think she ought to be made a Baroness in her own right." Then she recalls what particular haphazard activity was undertaken at that time. She took up

First Aid and Home Nursing or she acted in the Wizzlebury Pageant or she read the whole of *Paradise Lost*. She will remember how home life was going; she always seemed to be putting her foot in it with Daddy, or that was when she and Mummy first became such friends. Probably she still has an impression of the general run of weather. It was a fine summer and she can remember how her tennis improved and what lovely days in the country she and a girl friend spent. Or it was horribly wet and she took up music, but went to Paris just as she was getting on. Then there will be the exchequer. She never was so broke and simply lived in the upper circle but it was rather fun, or she was marvellously rich and bought that heavenly gentian-coloured dress and the gold cloak with one of those priceless collars and that darling flowered thing that made her look like a Dresden shepherdess, but never recovered from the storm at Ascot. (In any case there was, of course, a storm at Ascot.) Gossips with girl friends loom very large and in particular gossips with some best friend. Perhaps a temporary foible of the said friend, as a craze for Harold, or maybe the simple life, further dates the era. And there will be troubles and mortifications which are richly droll to look back on but which did not always raise a smile at the time. And there will always be a few time-honoured jokes belonging to any given period.

Young men, you see, do not loom so very largely when the thing is looked at in perspective. But if she has not leisure for such thoughtful and varied retrospect and wishes to bring back the past by a single image, the clue that gives it her is the name of a young man. "That was the year that Clive and I ran about together. Oh well!"

So with Claudia Heseltine. During her nineteenth year she saw Tintern Abbey for the first time. She found that she could draw caricatures and she and Eileen together did the Shakespeare festival at Stratford. During her twentieth year she spent April with the Northovers and discovered Max Beerbohm and A. E. Housman and, on returning to London, a really clever cheapish dressmaker. During her twenty-first year she made the acquaintance of the very smart and rather lovely Mrs. Noel Carstairs and through her managed to slide a foot, or half a foot, into the young married set. All these things seemed of enormous importance. None the less those years were for ever labelled Harry, Derek and Clive.

But that was before she knew Hugo Lester. Or saw Guy Verney. Or even heard that Lionel Byng played polo.

Claudia was an only child. She had had a brother till 1916; he had been much older than she and it was very long ago. Even her parents who loved him, liked him and were proud of him, did not really suffer from that loss as some would have suffered. They were happy in that they were a pair, dependent ultimately only on each other, in no way counting on that perennially broken reed, the next generation. Though they adored Claudia and she them and they all got on very well together, she used sometimes to feel with them as though she didn't really belong anywhere.

The Heseltines had a large, rather beautiful, quite modern house in the country and a flat in town. Mr. Heseltine, though business caused him to be in London several days a week, spent more and more time at the country house, using up his terrific energies in re-arranging and reorganising everything that he could. Mrs. Heseltine was generally there. She did not like travelling up and down. She was, she said, too fat. Sometimes she came to the flat for a prolonged spell of theatres and modistes (she dearly loved dress) but she was happier dispensing tea and lazy scandal to the county, or lying banked up with cushions as she skimmed some new novel. She was sociable and had a devoted, excellent housekeeper so she liked entertaining: more especially as it gave pleasure to her husband, providing him often with new suggestions for alterations, and sometimes with people who had the energy to argue.

Claudia did not really like country life. The country, yes. It was wonderful for visits. It gave her aesthetic pleasure and all sorts of stereotyped emotions. Sometimes up at the flat, safely sheltered and shut in with company and noise, she would yearn a good deal for the rain-washed green spaces, the yellow field flowers, and speak quite slightingly of the social engagements she had contracted. Yet for some nine months of the year only Saturday and Sunday, a rare Friday and a hunting Tuesday or so, ever lured her away from the flat. At country house parties she was always admirably tweeded and brogued and mackintoshed. But alone with her parents the week-end found her in a black tailor-made with a beige satin shirt, or a neat little crêpe de chine and lace affair, pottering round the lanes in thin, high-heeled shoes, or carefully making up her charming haggard face preparatory to birds'-nesting.

Claudia, when she considered the future at all, supposed that she would marry. But she seldom looked ahead and when she did she misdoubted her fate. She could only marry if she loved some young man and if he loved her too and if they loved each other at the same time, and really all that might never happen. Some people could marry from respect and affection, for suitability, community of tastes, safety and real worth. But this admirable course, so often successful, would never fit her temperament no matter how desirable it should appear. Therefore it was better not to think about the future as a continuous whole, but to live in the present and in that immediate future in which she had a contradictory and touching confidence. She liked to flirt a little and she liked people to be pleased with her. She did not want scalps; she disliked the attention or admiration of any man who was not himself attractive to her. All she tried to do really was to get and to give as much pleasure as might be.

With Eileen things were not in the least like that. She was a very definite person. She didn't stray from impulse to impulse, mild affair to mild affair. Nor had she any tendency, as had Claudia, to enjoy all things and condone all things. She knew her line and took it very completely.

Claudia was a thin, attractive-looking girl. Eileen was lovely. She had honey-gold hair, which by the way she *had* learnt to brush in Paris, and a small, classic profile. She could have been popular but she didn't want to; she wouldn't waste time playing agreeable, decorative games round dancing floors and race meetings, and she had a hard, uncompromising tongue. People who were allowed to get close to her at all got very fond of her indeed, but for the most part she kept a host of rather respectful mere acquaintances. She was cold and narrow and deep. She liked Claudia to pet her but never returned the caresses, she insisted on many letters but did not answer them much. She never repaid the host of small attentions which Claudia lavished on her and in which she took pleasure. But had they ever quarrelled, Claudia could have hurt her more than she could have hurt Claudia.

At first she intended not to marry, and accordingly filled her life with absorbing, impersonal interests. She never felt a flicker of the usual intriguing, imitation love. When she met Tommy Reynolds she changed her mind once and for all and determined to marry him. No one was more surprised than Claudia when Eileen returned from a house party babbling girlishly about him. In due course he either took to babbling boyishly about her or to registering the most controlled and manly reserve; anyway, he was always turning up on her doorstep bowed beneath a weight of choice blooms and peppermints. He was the last person anyone would have expected her to choose or to conquer. He was a good deal older than she, he had been considered a confirmed bachelor, he was a rich man who did no work, he was a philanderer, he was a *malade imaginaire* who drifted about rather charmingly in a perpetual fever about his tummy. There was a good deal of opposition to the match in spite of his money and a certain popularity: she was but twenty, a year younger than Claudia, and had been considered the future wife of a future Prime Minister.

But the result of the combat was never in doubt for a moment.

"I know where I'm going, and I know who's going with me,'" sang Eileen.

And "'I know who I love,'" finished Claudia, "'but the de'il knows who I'll marry!'"

3

← →

Only they see not God, I know,
Nor all that chivalry of His,
The soldier saints who, row on row,
Burn upward each to his point of bliss.
                                    BROWNING.

Claudia had motored Eileen down from London for a week-end at the Heseltines' country house. Tommy Reynolds couldn't come, so it was to be a week-end of perfect peace with no visitors. They found Mrs. Heseltine lying in a hammock near the rose garden. She had given way when quite a young woman to a distaste for exertion and a passion for cakes and cream. A beautiful skin and lovely blue eyes had survived the wreck of her figure.

"Claudia darling," she said, "do go and get me a glass of Kia Ora and the Boot's book from my bedroom. I know I'm always running you about and Eileen ought to take a turn now she's here, but she is so much more apt to grunt than you are when one asks her to do things, isn't she?"

As Claudia tripped off, Eileen smiled and said: "It's a mercy laziness doesn't run in the family, isn't it?"

"Well, you see, there's Fred to counteract it. He's reorganising the whole garden. You'll have to take an interest, Eileen. I really don't see that anyone else *can*."

By the time Claudia returned, her father had joined the party and was declaiming cheerfully in his rather hurried voice:

"No one but me takes the faintest interest in the place. Look at Amanda. If she were a woman of any resource she'd start a dairy or a hen coop or something and see after it herself. She could make it pay like smoke. That red-haired tenant's chimney smokes, he says. I shall have it seen to. Red hair's an extra charm on anyone good-looking, but absolute damnation, although ladies are present, to anyone who's plain to start with. All those children, and there are at least twenty-seven of them, have muddy skins and orange freckles. Extraordinary thing, heredity. I've noticed our little garden boy has just the same action throwing a dart that his father had who died before he can remember. Are any of you interested in the Mendelian theory?"

"None of us, darling," said his wife.

"I am really," said Eileen.

"You must come a walk," said Claudia, and led her away.

They wandered out without hats or coats or stockings and lay on the side of a hill. The sun soaked into them and a breeze ruffled their skirts and their hair.

"How did visiting Tommy's Mamma go off?" asked Claudia.

"Oh, very well. Ever since his father died she's lived in a charming country house with a twin sister she adores. They're exactly alike at first sight. Tommy said, 'One of these is my Mother. Of course I can't tell by merely looking, but we shall know later because she's the noisy one.' They amuse themselves by running the constituency. They're rather fun, a bit county but clever. He's very fond of them and likes being with them for short whiles, but too long at a stretch doesn't work because they press him to pudding, which the poor fool hates, and tell anecdotes about his school days when he didn't wash."

"Let's have a nice chat about Tommy," said Claudia.

Eileen grinned. "We'll hold off him while I can. I actually can at the moment and it seems an opportunity."

Claudia rolled over in the sun. "I am very happy," she stated.

"To-day is perfect," said Eileen, "one of the jolly things about childhood, an overrated time to my mind, was that at least one did live very much in the present. Now everything is mixed up with the past and the future. Don't you always wonder about the future?"

"Whether I'll go to Heaven and who I'll marry?" Claudia smiled. "No, I don't want to know. I just like to do what I feel moved to right away, and not lose the impulse of the moment, even if it's foolishness. 'S'attendre au lendemain n'est pas chose trop preste.'"

"It's jolly to live in the present like you do," said Eileen, "but you overdo it. There should be some pattern in life. People will drift till they come to a point where they have to choose and neither way seems very good. They take one and wish they'd taken the other, but never think of regretting the path they would follow till those were the only two inevitable alternatives."

"Don't be so signally strong-minded," complained Claudia.

Eileen thought a bit and began again. "One gets happier and pleasanter as one gets older," she said, "but I believe Wordsworth was right and one does lose some of the vision and the dream."

"Oh yes," agreed Claudia, "there is something divine about awkward, dumb and morbid young adolescents. So singlehearted and bursting with ideals. I wonder, was I like that and when did I change? The things one used to rebel against that one accepts now! It's 'the contagion of the world's slow stain' I suppose. But it makes one better company."

"You do believe in God still and all that?"

"Yes, darling. But the will of God is too inscrutable to follow."

"There's a most rollicking prayer," said Eileen, failing perhaps in her search for *le mot juste*, "about 'God without whom nothing is strong, nothing is holy, grant us grace so to pass through things temporal that we finally lose not the things eternal.' I think that has nothing to do with a future life and is good for this world and for everybody."

"True. Very amiable people get sadly swamped by the things temporal."

"Even that would be all right," concluded Eileen, "if the things temporal were what they really wanted. But they don't know what they want, and wherever they get it's an accident. Then they blame it off on to God or luck. Poor fish."

"When I was a child," said Claudia politely, "I used to preach to Mustard Middley and Nanny and Startling and May. They didn't mind." She went on, "But I didn't want to be a parson. I had a theoretical passion for blood."

"I am told," Eileen informed her, "that the only English word the Papuan natives know is 'bloody' and that they use it on every possible occasion. That and 'goddam.'"

"Really? I read part of a novel the other day about a lot of red blooded, he-male Empire builders who spent their whole time riding from bungalow to what not saying 'no heel taps' and 'goddam.' It was by Rex Hungerford and was such meat for strong men that I decided he *must* really be the vicar's maiden aunt. You know, like when one reads that poem of Swinburne's where they foamed all over each other with passion and one can't help wondering whether he really ever kissed a girl in the whole of his life."

"I don't suppose he missed much if he didn't," said Eileen on a note of pessimism.

"I expect you know," said Claudia. "I'll just ask Tommy to make sure."

"You shut up," said Eileen crossly.

4

Your face is made aware
Of ardour and surprise;
The stars are in your hair,
The sun is in your eyes.

GERALD GOULD.

When Claudia Heseltine was rising twenty-two, two very important things happened. Eileen married Tommy Reynolds, tabooing all interest in his tummy and pushing him into bill-broking. Hugo Lester appeared on the scene.

Eileen's newly married state threw Claudia slightly more on to the companionship of her next two best friends, bracketed somewhere below Eileen and ahead of the rest. The more exciting of these was Mrs. Noel Carstairs, and the more intimate Lady Rosemary Crane. Rosemary was her own age, fond of her, hospitable, much blessed with this world's advantages, and intellectually stimulating. Claudia did not always want to be intellectually stimulated and considered many of Rosemary's intelligent friends, both male and female, to be ticks. Still, plenty were interesting and some were nice and it was always fun to meet artistic, literary, or, I am afraid, even titled celebrities.

Claudia was genuinely and permanently fond of Rosemary, but within limits she went on and off her. She would have been fonder of her had she looked prettier or been of a type that attracted men by graces other than the intellect. Rosemary could have been pretty: she was neither fat nor red nor awkward; she had nice hazel eyes, pleasant, nondescript features and what might have been attractive brown hair. But her hair was always dressed to look like a bundle of shavings and shed hairpins everywhere, she got herself up like an elderly lady's paid companion, and she left her sallow complexion, her freckles and her nails to God. Her cleverness, however, was quite genuine. She was an excellent amateur actress, she knew five languages and sometimes translated foreign books into English, she played the violin, she took a valuable interest in after care and in reformatories, and she could tell you, though it is to her credit that she generally didn't, a surprising amount about political economy. Withal, she was cheerful and sociable, liked parties, and giggled a good deal.

It was at Lady Rosemary Crane's that Claudia met Hugo Lester.

Hugo Lester looked on Rosemary as a thoroughly nice girl, but he mistrusted her parties owing to a healthy dislike for abnormalities. He was in a weak position with regard to these, for he was a young novelist himself. As soon therefore as he espied Claudia, in her ravishing new spring suit, trying to keep the haughty lip uncurled at a brilliant but otherwise not wholly desirable young Polish pianist who plied her with tea, he gravitated naturally towards her and plied her in his turn with foie-gras sandwiches.

"Hurrah!" said Hugo. "Somebody at last who doesn't live for her art."

"Oh, but I *do*!" cried Claudia. "I sculpt in green wax."

Hugo's disappointment was obvious and pathetic. He was quite brave about it, however.

"What do you sculpt?"

"Portrait busts," explained Claudia, "only of course in allegory. You for instance—to me, you are a bandicoot and that quaint little woodland floweret Dead Man's Tongue."

But Hugo was taken in no longer.

"You little beast!" he observed. "I knew I was right."

"Have it your own way," she sighed. "What do you do?"

"I write novels," he told her.

She entered into this and informed him: "I read them all, of course. Do tell me what you've written."

"Oh, I wrote a book called *Paid in Full* and one called *The House of the Fool*. My last was *Celia Remembered*."

Claudia dimly recollected having heard one or two of these well spoken of.

"Yes," she said encouragingly, "and did you write *The Good Companions* and *Portrait in a Mirror* and *Brief Candles* and *The Edwardians*?"

Hugo burst out laughing. "What do you think I am really? A stockbroker?"

She looked him up and down. Slight, clean-shaven, awake, amused, very, very young-looking. He had almost a girl's skin, and a childish, eager look in his green eyes.

"No, not yet," said Claudia, "just an Etonian!"

"You're the rudest person I've ever met," pronounced Hugo. "Give me back that foie-gras sandwich."

They chattered on, very happy and at ease together. But just before he had to leave, Hugo, who had a certain love of mischief, sought out Rosemary and made her promise to tell Claudia that he had indeed written the novels he laid claim to and to add that he took himself very seriously and was exceedingly touchy about them.

Rosemary gave Claudia the message and added to it much information of her own, such as that Hugo was twenty-four, was an only son, was quite well off and had charming parents who lived at their equally charming house in Gloucestershire. Claudia got *Paid in Full* and *The House of the Fool* from her library, and she bought *Celia Remembered*, for, being a new book, it was out. She enjoyed them all, thought them well written, interesting, full of ideas. Then came the question whether or not she should write to Hugo and tell him that she had not known his name or she would never have made that mistake at Rosemary Crane's. On the whole it seemed less forward to ask Rosemary to have her to meet him again.

Rosemary had them both to dine for a lecture at the Institut Français and put them next each other at dinner. On a sudden inspiration Claudia told him that, much as she had liked all his books, she had cared for his first one least and considered his last to be his best. It was not true. She really slightly preferred *Paid in Full*, his first novel, which had made his name. But she guessed that nothing is more galling to the author than to have his earliest book always singled out for praise, as though he had made no progress or had no more to say, as though his initial success had been a flash in the pan. Besides, Hugo was tired of *Paid in Full*, and *Celia Remembered* interested him still. The admiration she expressed for it was moreover genuine and intelligent, so he was much pleased and thought her an unusually gifted girl.

"What fun to meet you again!" presently said Hugo.

"It was a surprise to see you," said Claudia insincerely, "and hardly a pleasant one after all the floaters I made last time."

"I'm putting you into my next book as a typical Philistine," improvised Hugo.

She clasped her hands. "Oh if you only would! You don't know what a lot of harm it's done me getting mixed up with Rosemary. The word has gone round the night clubs that all Rosemary's friends have brains."

"You can easily live that down," he consoled her. "Don't admit, of course, that you read people like Hugo Lester, but surely if you say you don't often care for books but you don't mind Dornford Yates and Phillips Oppenheim in small doses …"

"Nonsense," she interrupted crisply. "We can't have the word going round the night clubs that I'm a half-baked nitwit. Of course I have to study reviews of all the new and right poems and novels and biographies so that I can pretend I've read the lot. Now I come to think of it, three years ago I told everyone I'd read *Paid in Full* and thought it overrated."

"Oh," cried Hugo, "I *am* flattered! I think that's a really nice compliment. Of course, you owed it me after the floater."

"It wasn't really a bad floater," she said; "at least not a mortifying floater, so that I shall look back at it on wakeful nights and break out into cold sweats. It's funny the ones one minds and the ones one doesn't. There's lots of awful ones I never turned a hair over. There was a man I thought was Lady Rattislake's second husband when he was her first so that I called him Lord Rattislake instead of Mr. Jessel throughout. And there was a man I tried so gently and considerately to choke off, obviously because I thought I wasn't good for his peace of mind, and all the time I was really simply a stalking horse. And yet I was quite miserable for ages at the recollection of ever such a harmless one. It was at a house party and there was a chap I was only very moderately attracted by who quite liked me and he said at tea, 'Will you play with me after and we'll take on Mary and Ted?' And I said 'I should love to,' and then I saw, and everybody else saw, that he'd really been speaking to the girl on my other side. It haunted me for months and months. I wish you'd put something in a book about floaters."

"It's been done rather well already in *Barren Leaves*. Don't you ever read anything, my dear child—except Hugo Lester?"

"Only the *Matrimonial Post*," she told him.

They got separated at the lecture but he kept leaning backwards or forwards at the amusing bits, which were many, to try and catch her eye and share the joke with her rather than his neighbours. She noticed that he had a very ready, not noisy, but incapacitating laugh which seemed to shake infectious gurgles out of him. She noticed a little trick of constantly smoothing back his sleek, coppery hair. She noticed that the fair, smooth face (did he really have to shave at all?) with its small, regular features, would have been insignificant but for its animation, its constant twinkle. She considered that he looked nearer sixteen than twenty-four.

5

← →

The youth towards his fancy
Would turn his brow of tan,
And Tom would pair with Nancy
And Dick step off with Fan;
The girl would lift her glances
To his, and both be mute:
Well went the dances
At evening to the flute.

A. E. HOUSMAN.

"Mummy," said Claudia one Sunday shortly after, "a young man came to tea with me a day or two ago and brought me the *Matrimonial Post*. What do you think of that?"

"Ungallant, even officious," suggested Mrs. Heseltine, "but *really* friendly. I should like to thank him myself. So few people consider we poor mothers nowadays."

"We'd had some joke about it so he thought he'd buy me one for fun, and he crept furtively up, very shamefaced, to the street vendor in Trafalgar Square and whispered in a small, abashed voice, 'Er— *Matrimonial Post*, please.' And the man yelled in a voice of brass, "'MATRIMONIAL POST"? CERTAINLY, SIR.' And poor Mr. Lester crawled off with every eye upon him, blushing audibly."

"Still, if he's found you a husband in it, it was worth it."

"Well, I haven't applied anywhere yet, Mummy. I've studied the requirements and I find that what the average man demands of a wife is that she should be refined, lovable and musical. Do you think it's any good?"

"You may be lovable and musical but—my poor child, let us think of all the good a spinster can do," said Mrs. Heseltine.

"I want Mr. Lester down for a week-end some time," suggested Claudia, "to finish our interrupted talk. Dad came in after about ten minutes intending to go out again at once, took a fancy to him, burst into talk about Russia, Galsworthy, mental defectives, football and the Government, and finally carried him off to his own den. Afterwards he said, 'Dear me, was that somebody who'd come to see you? Well next time you see him, get him to talk to you about the hire purchase system in America. He was most interesting about it. Talking of America ...' And so on."

"You'll get less chance than ever at the week-end," laughed her mother. "I'll do my best for you, but he'll only say 'But I think young Lester's interested in what I say, my dear.' The *Matrimonial Post*'s your only chance of contracting an alliance. And even so you're only rather lovable and it's a matter of opinion whether you're musical at all. Run away, darling, I think I might be able to sleep till dressing time."

She put out her small, beautifully shod feet on the fender, leant her head on a cushion, and closed her gentian eyes.

Claudia did not think it necessary to pander to her wishes.

"Darling," she said, "you're looking so pretty. I wish I looked like the early photographs of you."

And she fetched the album of family photographs, rather obscurely known as Madame Tussaud's, and turned the pages, commenting aloud.

"Me at the age of two. Nothing ever looked quite so like a pig—except a pig. ... How elegant you were just after you married! Quite lovely. It's a shame, it really is a shame to have put comfort before everything. ..."

Mr. Heseltine came in with an open book in his hand and announced his intention of reading aloud from Wordsworth. His wife said that oh dear, he had such dreadful taste in literature, always Wordsworth and the Bible and things like that if it wasn't Einstein; would somebody pass her her French book as no one could sleep through his reading aloud. Claudia gave her her yellow-backed novel and curled up on the floor, so without further encouragement Mr. Heseltine burst into "Tintern Abbey," giving it a restless, staccato quality wholly alien to the poet.

Claudia loved the poem, but he had got no further than:

> "That best portion of a good man's life,
> His little, nameless unremembered acts
> Of kindness and of love,"

when her mind wandered off into consideration of her parents. She took those lines for her text to start with. They were like that. Even if her father, now that he did less in the City and it was all really Uncle Bob, frittered his energy and his talents into some rather futile channels; even if her mother let her gifts stagnate in a somewhat selfish laziness. They were so hospitable, so generous, so patient with other people's muddles and perplexities. Different as they were, people could come to either of them for sympathy and comfort and be sure to get it, and, if they wished, some sensible advice too. People of their own age, that was. The advice of their elders generally appeared purely academic to the young. Some little communicating link between the generation seemed always to be lost. Or was it that the advice, that the experience of others, is bound to be useless; that everyone must work out everything for himself? It seemed a good Protestant point of view. She decided never to become a Roman Catholic. A phrase came into her mind, "the curse of Cassandra on us all." Her father's voice jerked on, her mother dozed, and she thought how jolly it was to sit there in front of the log fire.

Hugo Lester's first week-end at Chesnor, the Heseltines' country place, was a great success. There were not many young men whom on such short acquaintance Claudia would have had to a party consisting only of herself, her parents, Uncle Bob and Great-Aunt Belle. But Hugo enjoyed it and made himself extremely popular. He was a young man who really very much liked the society of his elders. He had with them very good, considerate, sometimes even formal manners, and yet a dash of light-hearted impertinence which seemed to go down very well. After all, who wants to be treated as though they were dead and mummified? Claudia, as her mother had foreseen, had her work cut out to get him to herself at all; for not only had he made a hit with Mr. Heseltine but he made another with Great-Aunt Belle, who insisted upon telling him the separate history of every ring and cameo and piece of old lace that she wore. Great-Aunt Belle was a Heseltine relation and rather a terror. She loathed Mrs. Heseltine and directed many pointed remarks at her, but that lady regarded her almost with affection as a curiosity of natural history.

It was of course right that Hugo should like and be liked by Claudia's relations. But it was all wrong that he should not definitely prefer her company to that of the older generations. She was a little annoyed with him until, in the course of a walk with Daddy and Uncle Bob after Sunday tea, a fit of exuberance came upon him and he urged that he and she should run away from the others and hide. The suggestion fortunately was made not far from a giant hollow oak. They dodged round it and climbed up inside until they could look out from the top and spy upon their elders. They speculated upon the baffled mystification of Daddy and Uncle Bob over their disappearance, until those two gentlemen, deep in converse about politics, money, wine and agriculture, had strolled past with no thought of them. Then Hugo scrambled down inside the tree and a rather dishevelled Claudia discovered that she was stuck. Ultimately, telling him earnestly to look the other way, she slid down flushed and scratched and laughing into his arms and twisted round to face him inside the hollow trunk. There ensued one of those brief moments that girls think about afterwards, and wonder if there is really anything to think of and if the man thought anything at all. A tense, excited, still moment, shuttered off from the scramble before and the almost immediate turning away to crawl out from the tree and run home over the fields.

Having run a little, they decided not to bother to overtake the older men. The light of the March day was ebbing in angry gashes across the western sky. In the east a young moon put forth tentative horns. They looked at these things in silence for a little and then walked on talking quickly and eagerly about nothing memorable at all.

6

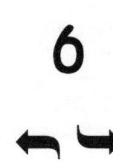

Life is a great mystery, indeed it is hard to see how it can be otherwise.

The Duke of Flamborough, Laurence Housman.

The summer that she was twenty-two passed pleasantly for Claudia, divided between Chesnor, country house visits and the flat in town. She spent much time at the flat, often alone and often with her father, occasionally with her mother too. Some advantages in Eileen's married state had now appeared. It was fun that Eileen had a house of her own, and Tommy was a dear. After all, as he was out of the way all the daytime bill-broking, his wife was often available as a companion to her old friend. Claudia had further to entertain her the usual engrossing affairs of her female friends, the usual new clothes, the usual round of gaiety, the usual mild nutters and diversions over attractive and attracted young men. And Hugo Lester had become a permanent feature of existence.

Hugo Lester had good manners. He would not throw over engagements for Claudia or even cut dances for her. Yet it gradually became clear that there was nothing that he was free to do for her that he would not do. She was not exacting; she never wished to come between anyone and his works or his friends. But it was soothing to think that Hugo's interest and admiration were to be relied upon; that he was there; that he was more hers than anyone's, and yet not really disquietingly hers, not dependent on her, so that she did not feel responsibility for him weighing upon her. Moreover he did her credit. His name was known, his work approved, and he was personally agreeable. It was a shame that he didn't care for dances, so that she seldom had the heart to drag him to them. But it was pleasant and flattering that he should so love to drop in to tea, talking so eagerly and confidentially, consulting her; he, who never told girls about himself. He would explain all about the film scenario he was writing, all about the new novel he planned, all about his profits, his commercial prospects in the immediate future. Always he would carry her away, kindle her too with his enthusiasm. He wanted her opinion about everything.

"Do you think this would be a good touch in my novel, just as one, slight reflection? You see there's this girl, this woman who's got to face her crisis. Shall she leave her husband or not? She's got to make up her mind and she can't make it up. She shuts herself in her room facing the problem in desperation, worn out with the mental suspense, her brain thrashing and churning around the for and against of either choice. If only she could settle it, and let irrevocable decision bring some sort of peace. And all the time that she is agonising over the choice, not knowing what she will do, not knowing to what she will turn the immediate future, some casual onlooker slightly involved in the affair, who has a rough-and-ready, thumb-nail mental sketch of her character, knows perfectly well, calmly, confidently, what she will finally decide to do. 'She won't leave her husband,' he says easily, 'she's not the type.' And after all her fever of uncertainty, of course she doesn't. She has to go through this hell of mental strife, and any passing acquaintance could tell the outcome long before with hardly a thought."

It was great fun discussing things, arguing, breaking down into laughter at their own disproportionate earnestness. Claudia was very helpful about female psychology, and was curious about male psychology in return. She was annoyed to find herself suspecting that he did not know so very much more about the latter than she did. Not as much more as he should. Say three times as much instead of sixteen times!

Hugo could not always be leant upon. He was dreadfully inadequate when their taxi driver stopped in the road after a dance at about one o'clock with the disquieting announcement: "I think there's someone dying in the road." He stood looking helpless and babbling about ambulances and police while Claudia raised and comforted a young woman who was writhing in the gutter. Only under directions did he manage to help support the stranger's sagging weight and guide her wavering steps to their taxicab. He could not help to elucidate anything from her when she was seated therein, but remained vaguely dismayed and upset while Claudia found out that she was uninjured, coaxed her address from her, and made the startling discovery that she was a German street walker strayed as it were from the pages of Galsworthy into real life.

"I hate them, oh I hate them!" she cried. "Schweinhund!" And then, defiantly, "You see, I'm German."

But Claudia could speak warmly of Germany. Pictures of her one trip there kept flashing across her mind. Dresden: wide, clean and spacious. Wienerschnitzel in the Drei Raben. A girl in a cabaret, Wally Winter her name was, dancing with a fair, loose-limbed man, doing a cross talk scene with him, finishing by cocking a snook, the one joke Claudia had understood. Nürnberg: its seven-storied roofs, its mediaeval turrets all alive and real to-day instead of being a well-preserved tourist show. Baireuth: the open-air café among the pines where you eat in haste waiting for the clang and the swell of the summons back for the next act of the opera. A picture post-card castle upon the Rhine and a great double rainbow over the river. Nightingales singing all the poetry in the world.

Claudia bundled Hugo into the taxi and gave the driver the lady's address. Then she sat with her arm round her, comforting her, for drink had made her sad. The German unfortunate kept making the most perfect, conventional remarks; that it was hard for those who'd lost their mothers, that she hated men, that she hoped Claudia wasn't disgusted by her, that Claudia was the sweetest thing she'd ever met. Occasionally she gave drunken cries of "Whoopee," trying to be brave as Claudia charitably decided, and once she began to laugh hysterically so that Hugo drew back and murmured, "My God," and Claudia cried sharply "None of that! You shut up!" before returning to her soft, sustained murmur of "There, dear, you'll soon be all right. It *is* hard. Poor dear. I think you're splendid. I think you're very brave. I'll look after you. It's all right, dear, now." They got her home at last and she kissed Claudia's hand and disappeared into the dark of her doorway with the parting words, "Good night, pal!"

"Ugh!" cried Hugo. "Thank God that's over. It made me feel quite ill."

"So I noticed," said Claudia mildly. "I wonder why? I didn't mind. Except that I'd always hoped till now that they liked it. Poor kid." And as the taxi carried her home to the flat she talked to Hugo very much on the lines of "there, dear, you're all right now."

Generally, however, Hugo was very invigorating. He was so interested about things and found everything either amusing or important. He and Eileen used to lecture her together about the importance of this and that. Eileen liked Hugo, though she regarded him vaguely as being far younger than she, and was delighted that he should bully Claudia about her really shameful ignorance of the politics of her country. Another day it was her insufficient interest in Rutherford's atom.

"It isn't only a question for scientists," he cried. "Don't you see how important it is to us all? Look at this table. I think it's thrilling, exciting, to realise that it isn't solid at all, that it consists of unattached particles set far apart from each other, held in place by the flow of electricity."

"I don't see what that matters to you," objected Claudia, "as long as the table is, in daily practice, solid enough for you to put your glass of port on."

He nearly exploded. "Don't you see? *Don't* you see all that it implies, the vistas that it opens up? I think the fact that this table isn't a solid object at all is the most wonderful and important thing in the world."

"How can you be so material?" urged Eileen. "Don't you see that if matter *isn't* matter ..."

They were almost in tears with their passionate earnestness.

"You two *are* more spiritual than I," admitted Claudia, "but I don't see what good it does anyone. I look on people as animals who can't help themselves, and so I am nice and unresentful and forgiving and kind. And you look on people as souls who *can* help themselves, and in consequence you are perfectly beastly about them and often to them. At least Eileen is. Eileen's always blaming her fellow kind."

"You can't be really angry unless you think things matter," explained Hugo.

Afterwards this conversation depressed her. She was always a little temperamental, gay go up and gay go down, in mood, and did not like to be long alone. She felt that she was getting material and unspiritual. Tables to her were things to put port on, people creatures to be given port to, and her highest ideal to share her very best port with all. Port or bread or flowers or anything else that you could put on a solid table for warm, breathing, human animals. And the unsolidarity of matter— the proton, the electron, the electricity that were the foundations of all matter—left her unmoved.

Claudia enjoyed herself very much. She was gay, she was content. But she was not exactly very happy this year that she was twenty-two. She was apt to feel lonely, to be afraid of feeling lonely, to be appalled by the barriers that cut us off each from each. She was loved and happy in her home, but her father and mother were one, an entity of their own, she had no real niche there. She and Eileen clung to each other, but had she really any natural, enduring place in Eileen's lot? Seven men in her life had wanted to marry her, seven more might want to do so, but when they tried to come suddenly nearer, at once a pleasant, transient relationship was shattered and they were suddenly worlds away; strangers who thought her cruel not to give them something that she had not got to give. It would be intolerable if that happened with Hugo; he had become such a habit, such a refreshment.

Why had she got to justify an existence she had not sought? How did one become better than one was already? She was a satisfactory daughter, she minded about the feelings of others, she was scrupulous with her tongue. She gave her tithe to charity and she stuck to the (to her) loathsome good works with which Rosemary Crane, catching her off her guard, had landed her. Material, material! Glasses of port on a solid table! But she was never introspective for long, and generally concluded with the thought that she did at least succeed in enjoying herself, and many girls with equal opportunities didn't even do that. Why change at all when you do enjoy yourself, and your friends like you as you are, and you, to be honest, are very fond of yourself?

As to the future, why anticipate? It will come when it must, and then we shall see.

7

⬅ ➡

On aime d'abord par hasard,
par jeu, par curiosité,
pour avoir dans un regard
lu des possibilitiés.

GÉRALDY.

Mrs. Noel Carstairs may or may not have been a good friend for Claudia. She was certainly a good friend to her. She must moreover have been fond of her. Granted that she was rich and loved entertaining so that a few attractive girls were necessary to balance unmarried men, granted that in her set it was always Christian names and dear and darling and signing letters with love from the very start, there was still no reason why she should have been so constant in her kindness to her.

Lalage Carstairs had golden-brown eyes, hair red like beech leaves, a lined, animated face and the prettiest small figure in the world. She was a little spoilt, a little vague, a little affected, priding herself on impulsiveness, unpunctuality and absence of mind. She hated to be alone and was easily bored, but on the other hand no one was more readily amused and distracted. An S.O.S. from Lalage, finding life tedious, was never an effort to rise to. She was charming in appearance, chic, vivacious and extremely generous, so that it really is a question whether her friends would not have liked her nearly as much as if she had not been so hospitable and so rich.

One winter day Claudia arrived in a thoroughly bad temper to dine for a dance with Lalage. She had asked Lalage if she might bring Hugo, which had perhaps been cool of her. Then Hugo had said that he really could not stand young married and youngish married parties, and that Lalage's friends were noisy, unmoral and common to a degree that in his opinion they could not carry off merely by being nice-looking, well dressed and smart. So she had quarrelled with Hugo, not because he wouldn't come (he would have come if she had been firm with him) but because he had been unkind about her friends. Then she had had to ring up Lalage and beg her, in a small voice, to provide a partner for her after all. And now she wished she had rung up Hugo nicely at dressing time, not that it had been much of a quarrel but that she was unused to quarrelling with anyone, let alone with him. It seemed so unnatural that there should have been a serious, guarded moment between her and Hugo.

But Lalage was soothing. Lalage thought she looked delightful. Lalage had had no difficulty in securing Guy Verney without his wife. Hadn't she wanted to put off Claudia and have Mrs. Verney? Oh no! As a matter of fact Carol couldn't come, but in any case she was impossible, my dear, impossible. Darling Guy had married Carol by mistake. It was odd as he was cold and not susceptible. But then she was lovely. An actress. Claudia was much intrigued.

Guy Verney sat on one side of Claudia at dinner and was nice, but he was more occupied with Mrs. Derek Denzel on his other side and Claudia with her old friend Noel Carstairs on hers. Dear Noel, tall and fair and happy, who having long ago decided that she was amusing was automatically and genuinely overcome with mirth at everything she said. Later Guy Verney danced with her once and made her feel successful and at ease, but he did not stay long with the party, going off to the Embassy fairly early with Lord and Lady Alcester and Lady Gilda Cazlitt who had brought one Alan Vane instead of her husband to the dance.

It was a pleasant party. Claudia clicked unsubstantially just for the evening with Alan Vane, who had scorned the Embassy detachment and was very pleased with himself for the way he had asserted his independence with Gilda Cazlitt. He confided a lot of his love affairs to Claudia, and she resurrected some to confide to him, and she really quite hoped that next time they met he would at last manage to recognise her without being reminded.

Lalage and Noel ultimately saw her home. Lalage said:

"Guy told me you dance very well. He liked your frock."

She was surprised and delighted. She had been rather impressed by Guy, not so much because she discerned anything special about him as because all the other women had seemed to be impressed and she was susceptible to mass suggestion. And Guy had liked them, admired them, enjoyed talking to them, and had not been impressed. He was not susceptible and he was cold. Somehow she had felt that Lalage was right about that. He wouldn't be ensnared by any of these idle, ensnaring creatures. And yet he didn't feel at all like Hugo; no more than like Alan Vane with all his gay, decorative flirtations. Nor had he seemed, somehow, like a married man. She felt a little fascinated by him, and curious about the lovely actress wife. It seemed so romantic of him and she did like lovely women.

"I liked him," she told Lalage. "I wonder why I haven't met him before with you? And oh, Lalage, I *would* like to meet the impossible Mrs. Verney!"

"All in good time if you want to, but I assure you she's pretty ghastly," laughed Noel.

She went to bed in high spirits. She had looked nice. She had got on well with everyone. She had clicked with Alan Vane whom she very much admired. She had met a new man who was rather intriguing. She was going to meet a ravishingly lovely, impossible ex-actress. And to-morrow she'd ring up her dear Hugo and tell him that he had been quite right, he'd have loathed it, and that—live and let live!—she wouldn't grudge him his dislikes.

8

← →

Who would not give,
If so he might, to duty and to truth
The eagerness of infantine desire?
                    WORDSWORTH.

The Christmas party at Chesnor was a duty or family one, only diluted
and enlivened by the presence of Eileen and Tommy Reynolds. Great-
Aunt Belle was in good form, and after the usual unpleasantness over
her presents (for those she received were bound to strike her as being
either mean themselves or deliberately calculated by their ostentation to
make hers to others look mean—generally the latter) she brightened the
proceedings by asking when Fred and Amanda were going to ask that
young Lester fellow's intentions about Claudia. Mr. and Mrs. Heseltine
explained that they had thought of it, but that she was a sensible girl
who knew her own business and she was maybe marking time while
she looked for a title. Tommy imported further acidity into the party
by confiding in Great-Aunt Belle, in a burst of wholly misplaced
sprightliness, that Eileen was one of those modern wives a fellow saw
nothing of, and that her temper was such he simply daren't ask her
what she did with her evenings. Great-Aunt Belle took his side with
unforeseen energy.

Hugo's present to Claudia, the occasion of Great-Aunt Belle's attack,
arrived actually on Christmas Day and consisted of all the books of

André Maurois nicely bound to match. A cheap present would have delighted her just as much, but since it was an expensive one she found entertainment in totting up the price and boasting of it to herself. It was not as if Hugo were extravagant either. But that of course was just childishness. The main thing was that he had thought of her, because this gave her a sense of companionship. And after Great-Aunt Belle's outburst she thought of his voice, saying that she must come and stay for a week-end with his people when it could be arranged. There had been nothing remarkable in what he had said, but there had been some rigid, breathless quality in the way he had said it. She had dissipated it promptly in a flow of chatter. She did not want anything to happen between them. She did not want to reorganise her life for Hugo, but she certainly could not face the prospect of losing him.

They all went to church of course. Mrs. Heseltine and Claudia generally went on Sundays, Mr. Heseltine went every Sunday and read the lessons. To-day being not Sunday but Christmas Day, church attendance was almost compulsory. Claudia would have gone in any case, but as sometimes happened to her she felt that she wanted to go.

The cold grey church of St. James's had suddenly become very naïve and gay. At the west end there was a model crèche. The light of an artificial star flooded warmly down on to the ox and the ass, the blue and white Madonna with her lily in her hand, the trusting, kind St. Joseph, the manger, the strawed floor, and the baby Himself with wide-stretched arms and wide-open eyes. At the east end, beside the altar steps, real live Christmas trees tapered and pointed up, hung with painted glass baubles, tinsel frilled crackers and coloured paper festoons. The altar itself seemed to blaze with its serried heaps of flowers. Holly and mistletoe jauntily climbed up the rails of the chancel screen.

There was a good congregation. The choir and the priest entered as to a burst of applause on the exultant notes of "Hark the herald." Claudia felt rather emotional. Of course that was not religion (any more than feeling choky at "Abide with me," or saying "God bless you!" with a lump in the throat!) but it was rather pleasant. At first the whole thing seemed very triumphant and glorious and big. And then later on it suddenly seemed very simple and touching, something you wanted almost patronisingly to protect. Very holy—but so frail. Of course that wasn't the right way to feel. "Once in royal David's city …" And then there was a very good sermon. And she began to feel that perhaps it was she who was defenceless and little. One ought to be able to do more about it than one did. It was not sin that Christ condemned nearly so much as stupidity. People need not be so stupid, so unperceptive, so dead. Seeing, they *would* not see; hearing, they *would* not understand. So Christ tried, not to reform, but to wake them up. And He never regarded the body as divorced from the spirit, or of no account. He never despised flesh. He gave the people wine at Cana of Galilee, and when He spoke of the spirit He used the concrete image, saying to Simon Peter, "Feed My lambs."

> "Oh come, all ye faithful,
> Joyful and triumphant,
> Oh come ye, oh come ye
> To Bethlehem!"

The organ blared, the congregation shouted; how they all let it rip! "Come ye, oh come ye—" If they only could! To the child in the stall at Bethlehem, like children at this children's festival. Children were little demons, dirty, rough and unkind. But one looked back startled on a time when one was so single-hearted. And so very innocent. Claudia marvelled anew at the mystery of how grown people with their complexes, their repressions, their mixed motives and tangled desires, could ever have been as that stocky, sturdy child two pews ahead who had just dropped three hymn books to the floor and was fidgeting beside its nurse. And there in church, singing "Oh come ye, oh come ye …" it did seem suddenly inappropriate and unfitting that people should be hard to each other or that they should condemn. Thus vaguely moved she put more than she had intended in the collection plate.

The Heseltines got up a good deal of Christmas spirit and there was a certain amount of fun available in the county. There was notably an excellent dance at a house some fifteen miles from Chesnor, and the Heseltines' children's party, a time-honoured social event which took place with great success almost every Christmas; that is whenever Claudia spent Christmas at home. In the course of January there were the Farmers' Ball, the Hunt Ball and the Kennedy-Rye's Bottle Party, and what with these and various country house visits Claudia felt that she had been long absent from the dear old home by the time she settled down again to life at the flat every Monday to Friday or Saturday.

She was sitting one day in the pleasant drawing-room of the flat going through her post, with Hugo perched on the arm of her chair calmly looking over her letters. She opened one from Rosemary Crane, and presently began to laugh.

BELOVED CLAUDIA, the letter began,—Such an unexpected annoyance! I dined for a fancy dress ball and I was introduced to rather a good-looking man whom I thought was Dion Dring the artist. Well we got on awful well, and you know what it is with the carnival spirit and being all painted up as Cleopatra and looking so preternaturally devastating for once and the way I can't help giggling at parties, I found we'd got to the end of the evening with never a word of sense and nothing said about Art at all. So I bubbled spontaneously out with an invitation for a week-end at Aston Cobalt. He immediately accepted. My dear, what *shall* I do with him? It was Lionel Byng!

"Who's Lionel Byng?" asked Claudia.

"Really, my poppet," protested Hugo, "you should read the papers. He's much more in your line than mine. He's the famous polo player."

"Oh *that* fellow! Lucky Rosemary—I should like to meet him. But I needn't worry and neither need she. An important man like that is certain to chuck a weekend accepted on impulse after a good evening!"

"Talking of week-ends," said Hugo, "you must come and stay with us in Gloucestershire. I've suddenly thought it would be nice if you'd come for my birthday. Have you got a calendar? I know the date but I can't remember the day of the week. I want to fix it now. You *must* come."

"I can't find a calendar. What's the date to-day? We can count up."

"I can't remember," said Hugo.

"Oh well, never mind," decided Claudia, "I know I can come. I'm only booked for next week-end that's important. There's nothing else I couldn't get out of for a thing like your birthday."

"That'll be wonderful," he told her, and smiled a quick, radiant smile. "When we're up there it'll be a good place, I mean it's lovely, and there'll be time, well anyway, I'll write you the date as soon as I get home and make sure it's all right."

He wrote to her the following morning. She found his letter and another from Rosemary waiting for her as she let herself into the flat between tea and time to dress for dinner. She opened her letters and read them in the hall, then went towards the drawing-room to answer them at once. As she opened the door, the telephone started ringing.

There was a fire in the room; very comforting and gay. It threw a lovely liquid sheet of orange on the big armchairs on each side of it. It sent a flickering glow on to the gallery table where lay weekly and daily papers, magazines, a few books lately thrown down. The cushions were fluffed out, inviting. An antique clock marked time in a hushed monotone. Only the fire was alive, consuming its life—for what?

PART III

TURNING TO THE LEFT

1

If you start worrying what girls see in ginks, your mind's going right off your business.

On the Spot, EDGAR WALLACE.

There was no one in the room. Blinds and curtains were closed; the light of the skies, if any, was shut out. Branches and trails of flowers stood in great jars, drained of their colour in the shadows but not of their faint sweetness. The door opened and as Claudia came with hurried steps into the fire's glow, two open letters in her hand, the telephone began ringing. She shut the door and turned up the lights.

She crossed to the writing-table, threw down the letters and lifted the telephone receiver.

"Hullo … yes of course it is, Lalage dear … yes, longing to meet him again and the dazzling actress … how sweet of you … oh, dear, but I can't! Not the week-end after next. … I can't really, I'm going to Gloucestershire. … What fun the party sounds. … No I really can't possibly … darling, I tell you I can't … Oh Lalage, but I can't really!" It flashed suddenly across her mind how very much she would enjoy this party, even apart from her desire to see again the intriguing Guy Verney. And on a sudden impulse, speaking quickly lest she change her mind again, she cried, "Listen, darling. I *will* come. … Yes, I'd love to. I'll fix it somehow … I must come, it sounds such fun! You're a lamb to ask me. … Bless you and a thousand thanks … yes … yes … all right … Lovely! Good-bye."

She sat down at the desk and wrote:

DARLING ROSEMARY,—How sweet of you and I'd have loved it! And I wanted to meet Lionel Byng! But I can't possibly, I'm week-ending with the Carstairs at Farling. Isn't it too damnable? Ever so many thanks and I *am* sorry. Let's ring each other up on Monday.

Your loving
CLAUDIA.

Then she turned to her second letter: DEAREST HUGO,—she began, I *am* sorry, and I'd love to come absolutely *any* week-end after. But I got in a frightful muddle … It was a difficult letter to write, and she felt rather caddish as she finished it.

The party at Farling consisted of the Cazlitts, the Denzels, the Alcesters, Lord Rattislake who had been Mrs. Delmar Vermont's second husband, Miss Slade who was in a dress shop, Alan Vane, the Verneys, and of course Claudia and the Carstairs themselves. Alan Vane, complete with car and chauffeur, took Claudia down on the Thursday evening. She cross-questioned him about Carol Verney. He said, as usual, ever charitable, that she was a little darling and a sweet little thing. Was she pretty? Yes, very. Was she clever? No. Was she amusing? Only late at night when she'd drunk a little. Was she nice? Oh, well, she was a nice little thing. Claudia wanted to ask whether Alan respected her but decided not to in case he didn't. She liked all women to be respected even in defiance of reason. They returned instead to that perennial source of interest to social London, Alan's love affairs. She was amused and sympathetic, and towards the end of the journey let him hold her hand, excusing to herself her unaccustomed conduct on the obscure ground that Alan didn't count.

All such women of the house party as knew Claudia already, greeted her after the peculiar way of their set: that is, with an enthusiastic warmth which they did indeed feel at the moment, and with many pleasant plans for clasping her to their bosoms in all their future doings and taking her everywhere, whereas, in fact, only Lalage ever asked her to anything. Not such a bad peculiar way either. Claudia knew that she was not really one of them, that they would forget her again. Meanwhile they spoke sincerely, it made her one of them for the moment and caused her to feel good.

Only three of her fellow guests were unknown to her. Lord Rattislake, who was still generally admitted to be a good fellow, but whose good looks were now running to flesh and dissipated lines. Miss Slade, who was unbelievably slender without being thin, and who possessed brown velvet eyes and a husky voice. And Mrs. Guy Verney.

Carol Verney was beautifully made, a little plump, and the happy owner of the most wonderful golden curls. She never came down before twelve, and lounged about all day in rapturous Ascot creations, carefully enamelled, laden with jewels, and smelling like a hothouse full of flowers. One was relieved to find that she had the voice of a lady, but a lady who affected a drawl. She hardly roused herself to talk to the other women at all and seemed to think that looking at her should be sufficient even for the men; that is until after dinner, when having drunk a really surprising amount, a feverish vivacity would grip her, an edge would come into the drawl, and she would roll her great grey eyes and gesticulate with her heavily ringed hands, laughing shrilly and telling an endless variety of funny stories with an air of curiously innocent corruption.

"He never saw her in the daytime till after he married her," explained Lalage, less kind than Alan. "They met every night after the theatre and she carried him completely off his feet. She never gave him time to pull himself together. You must remember photographs of the wedding. A terrific splash, and she had groomsmen as well as bridesmaids. Marrying a gentleman, and one with money, has gone completely to her head. The airs she gives herself, and the way she treats Guy!"

She was always trying to quarrel with Guy, always attacking him, and though he did not perhaps seek her company he was invariably considerate and courteous. Claudia was appalled at her constant aggression, till she suddenly thought: "God help her! She's trying to assert herself. He doesn't love her any more and she loves him still."

But Lalage said that she was known to be unfaithful to him and probably took drugs. And she added more kindly: "Poor Carol! I suppose it's bad luck partly. Very few married couples are as happy as Noel and I."

All the women of the party were nice to Carol and Sir Reggie Cazlitt discovered in her, temporarily, his ideal of womanhood. It was a party which tended to fall into couples, and as it started on Thursday evening, for some of the men wanted to hunt on Friday, there was time for plenty of alliances to shape and reshape. It was perhaps in self defence that Guy singled out Claudia. The Farling party was his natural element, the other women his friends whose companionship he regularly sought. But they always wanted to start something; they had designs upon his mental independence which he invariably evaded. Claudia was a nice little thing with no designs. He was fourteen years older than she and felt quite avuncular, he told himself; while at the same time her immaturity was rather rejuvenating. It was a novelty to get to know something so innocent, so inexperienced. Yet she was not a débutante and knew quite well how to dress and how to behave.

And Guy himself? What did anyone see in him? He was an ordinary enough man of thirty-seven, very well-made, six feet one or two in height, with dark hair, grey-blue eyes, a thin, sallow face and protruding front teeth. Women liked his pleasant voice with its slightly cynical sound, his friendliness and his aloofness, his tolerant, selfish way. Men liked his ability to do the usual sort of thing well, to talk easily and to suit himself to his surroundings. He carried on successful financial operations with two partners in the neighbourhood of Liverpool Street Station. His one distinctive accomplishment was playing with great dexterity on the banjo and singing almost any amusing song you could think of with a rather pleasing, matter of fact air. He was a very civilised product with sophisticated tastes and a simple mind. He wished himself all possible good and no one any harm.

Perhaps it was really Claudia who took the initiative. She felt from the start that it was not for nothing that she had noticed him, remembered him, so particularly. Somehow it was very important that they should be friends. Not only for her vanity's sake. It was natural and right. It was fated. She had a responsive nature, and friendship, with a capital F or perhaps even with two small ffs, was her ideal. And being such an eminently harmless little creature she was able to worm her way under his guard and stake out her claim.

Guy and Claudia were returning from a walk after tea on the Sunday. It was nearly dark. They had suddenly ceased talking.

"You're looking very solemn," said Guy.

They were nearly at the house. They paused and looked in silence on the February dusk. They saw the holly, an opaque hillock of darkness; the birch, a blurred plume; the cedar, horizontal layer upon layer of frayed black. In the sky behind the holly was a last smudge of colour forgotten from the day, a rusty smudge, a faded bloodstain filmed over with a wash of grey. Through the cloudy curtain across the sky's space, nine stars, three bright, six dim and struggling, showed their remote faces.

"Why are you solemn?" asked Guy in a quiet voice.

Claudia's answer was hardly an answer. "It's been such a nice week-end."

He agreed; "Yes it has. Very."

"You've enjoyed it too, then?"

"Yes of course I have. You've been so terribly nice to me."

"But now it's over, Guy."

"Not till to-morrow."

She said reproachfully: "Aren't you going up to-night after dinner with Alan?"

– 59 –

"But to nowhere less remote and accessible than London," he consoled her.

Claudia drew a sharp breath. "Shall I see you in London then?"

"Yes of course." He considered a moment. Perhaps he ought not to take her out dancing. But some suggestion was clearly called for. "You say you like racing. Will you join the little party we were talking of? We want another woman, and I'll arrange it all and call for you."

"Oh! I'd love you to," she answered. "Thank you, Guy."

"That'll be lovely," he assured her, "and now let's come out of this very depressing twilight." He took her arm in a firm grip and steered her briskly to the house.

2

← →

"Do you know Hugo?"
"Hugo who?"
"Hugo to hell!"

OLD SPANISH PROVERB.

Croyez-vous aussi, me dit-elle, qu'il soit si facile d'être jolie fille
sans causer de malheurs?

ANATOLE FRANCE.

Two things happened before the racing party took place. The Verneys
had a terrific row, ending in the departure of Carol for Hollywood.
Hugo came to call on Claudia.

"Had a nice week-end?" asked Hugo.

"Yes, awfully. Oh Hugo, I am sorry about it! I'd simply love to come
any other time—though I notice you haven't asked me!"

"I can't wait till then. You knew, didn't you, what I was going to say
last week-end? Or did you not know? Which was it?"

It came to her unpleasantly that actually she must have known, but
just hadn't thought about it. She couldn't answer, "I forgot," so she
answered instead: "I didn't realise."

And she looked pleadingly at Hugo where he stood close before her
chair, young and boyish and very slight, his smooth, almost girlish face
creased with anxiety.

She thought absurdly: "I wish he were my son." And she began to talk.

"Won't you sit down? You're not in a hurry, are you? You look so restless, my dear, hovering about like a bird on the wing, you quite unnerve me. How have you been writing these last few days?"

He didn't sit. He remained standing before her, fidgeting like a schoolchild with his hands. He said:

"You could make me write, Claudia, I know it's in me to write good books. But these last days I could write nothing for thinking of you. I think I've always loved you, but now it's different; I'm in love with you and I can't bear it. Darling, I do make you happy; you'll never be able to talk to anyone easier than you can to me. Marry me, Claudia, marry me please, and I'll write you the best books in the world. I'll make you happy, I love you so."

It was worse than she could have believed possible. She longed to give him all he wanted. He was so very dear, and yet he was somehow remote, ineffectual, a ghost out of something that had ceased to be. She began to falter the time-honoured stuff about his trying not to think of her like that, and being sorry, and so fond of him in a different way. And as his face became hurt and lost and desolate he looked younger than ever, less than sixteen, a little boy of eight. After they had gone through the dreadful rigmarole about hoping and not hoping, he went on standing helplessly there, looking round the room with a trapped, distasteful gaze, unable to go.

"I thought you were fond of me," he said at length.

"How I led him on!" she told herself. Aloud she said:

"I am, I am, but oh Hugo, not that way." And she cried, "I wish I could marry you! I don't know what's the matter with me. I shall probably never know anyone so nice again."

She looked at him with something of his own helpless supplication, as though asking him to be strong and competent, a solid fact in the present, instead of dematerialising almost visibly into thin air.

"Couldn't you ever? Oh Claudia, couldn't you try?"

"Never, never. It just isn't any good,"

Still he didn't go. She said:

"We can be friends all the same, can't we, Hugo?"

He shook his head hopelessly.

"I don't think we can, darling."

And he went at last, rather stunned, for in his heart he had felt confident of Claudia.

Hugo didn't go to Hollywood but he went round the world.

3

Demain! Il fut un temps où ce mot contenait pour moi la plus belle des magies. En le prononçant, je voyais des figures inconnues et charmantes me faire signe du doigt et murmurer: "Viens!" J'aimais tant la vie, alors! J'avais en elle la belle confiance d'un amoureux, et je ne pensais pas qu'elle pût me devenir sévère, elle qui pourtant est sans pitié.

ANATOLE FRANCE.

In March Claudia became twenty-three and throughout her twenty-fourth year she possessed a new, calm, unaccountable happiness. It seemed that all the waste corners of her life flowered before the friendship with Guy.

Why shouldn't they be friends? She asked herself to lunch with him once or twice in the city at the Great Eastern after the racing party. When summer came she got up tennis fours in the evening. Then he began to take her to theatres and dance places like anyone else. She knew quite well that he went out with all the others, for the two of them used to compare their news and tell each other anything amusing they'd done. It would not have been her fault if he hadn't known that she had plenty of other men friends. So they became mutually a habit, pleasant and soothing. Eileen disapproved of it all very much. The Heseltine parents knew Guy Verney's name as a married friend of Claudia's and Lalage's, even met him once and liked him.

Claudia told herself that she was deceiving them and yet she did not feel that she was. Life at the flat always was shuttered off from life at Chesnor. She kept them as it were in different boxes.

Claudia was pleased when Alan Vane confided to her bits of his so-called private affairs. When Guy did so at last she was more than pleased; it really was ffriendship with two small ffs, because he didn't tell things to the others. She never forgot one evening over a table for two at the Savoy when she made him tell her how he had been engaged to be married to a charming and lovely woman at the time he had met Carol. He suddenly felt that Claudia might understand, or alternatively that she wouldn't understand and it wouldn't matter. So he told her how at one meeting with Carol, at first sight, his engagement had blown up. His charming and lovely woman had married a rotter on the rebound and gone with him to India. He said unhappily:

"We did so mean to love each other for ever."

Claudia thought not of her but of Carol. For when he married her they too must have meant to love each other for ever. Poor Carol, turning a new page in dazzling white with a flower garland for the sacrifice on her coronal of golden curls.

He told her, "We used to meet after the theatre, and she was so vital and gay. Just occasionally she was wistful. She thought she wanted a home." Then he began again suddenly: "You know that line 'For each man kills the thing he loves'? It's perfectly true. If he loves an experienced woman he wants to make her innocent; if he loves a pure one he wants to teach her all about the world." He laughed suddenly. "Don't look so grave! Come and dance."

All through the year, from time to time, little inconsequent vignettes of him etched themselves with peculiar reality on her memory for ever. Guy walking in the Park with her in October on a cold day, saying anxiously that her coat wasn't warm enough.

"Pooh! It's got to do the winter; it's the only warm coat I've got."

"Let me get you a thick one. Please, I should like to. ... Don't be silly, Claudia, there's no sort of nonsense like that between you and me. I can buy you one so easily, and I hate my friends to be cold!"

She had protested that she had all the money in the world and was too hot already, but he had made her run, laughing and panting, over the grass to keep warm. Guy, after tennis in the summer with his white shirt open: she could call to mind so vividly the set of his head and neck. Guy comforting her when she had read in the papers of the death in the street of a sodden old flowerwoman she had sometimes dealt with, who, it appeared at the inquest, had once been the famous Lou Delane. Because it was dreadful that someone you had actually met should die. And it was dreadful that a triumphant music-hall star could become a blear-eyed hag selling flowers in the street. And it was most dreadful and pitiful of all that death should vanquish one who had once, as the papers told, had all those jewels, all those debts, all those lovers, and been the toast of fashionable men in London, Paris and New York. Guy had been perfect about it. When younger he had even heard of her from older men. The famous high kick, the famous turn of the head when she said: "Hullo boys! How *are* you all this evening?" The famous auburn hair. He had taken Claudia's hand with infinite gentleness, infinite precaution. It was the December after they had met and it was the first time they had held hands.

Claudia was to him something fragile and to be protected. He was especially anxious that when she married it should be someone of whom he approved. In the early days he even produced a few eligibles for her. On rare occasions he suddenly decided for the moment that he was not a good friend for her and urged the fact upon her. She retaliated by laughing at his conceit in supposing himself to be dangerous. They felt very easy and natural and affectionate together, and it became necessary to be together often.

When Carol came back from Hollywood she lived in Guy's house, but she was in no one's way for she had a theatre engagement as leading lady and hardly saw her husband at all. Guy and Claudia met often. But never again by invitation of Lalage or any of her set. Even though they were Guy's own set. Even though Lalage persisted in her kindness and hospitality to Claudia so that some of the others, through meeting her often, took her up too. They knew of her success with Guy for they teased him about it, but never by any accident were the two asked out together.

A radiance and secure happiness hung about Claudia in all her doings, in all her ways. It made her prettier than she had ever been and could have ensured her a dazzling supply of all the attentions she loved. But it was impossible to concentrate on other men.

4

← →

What, not upbraid me
That I delayed me,
Nor ask what stayed me
So long? Ah no!—
New cares may claim me,
New loves inflame me,
She will not blame me,
But suffer it so.

HARDY.

I didn't say there was nothing better than hay, I said there's
nothing like it.

Alice Through the Looking-Glass.

One Friday, Eileen and Claudia motored down together to Chesnor.
Tommy was to join them the next day.

"Hullo, Eileen," said Mrs. Heseltine, delighted to see her favourite
guest, "we've had a terrible misfortune. Fred has started pigs and there's
no peace or quiet for anyone. You're fond of dumb animals, aren't you?"

Eileen smiled. "Oh yes, very. Do I have to fraternise with them?"

"Well, you watch them woffling their swill and ask Fred leading
questions on pig culture. You could read up ham-curing in the

Encyclopaedia of an evening when you cut out at bridge. Don't let Fred rush you into keeping a pig in your Square Gardens. Fred is so impulsive."

"I'm now going to take the girl friend for a walk," announced Claudia.

When they were slogging it across the fields, "I suppose you are still Guying it up and down?" asked Eileen. The discussion was a departure. She would have liked to have had the key of all Claudia's affairs, but her own reserved, uncommunicative attitude unwittingly discouraged confidences. Thus challenged, however,

"Yes, I am Guying it," said Claudia, "down rather than up."

"Meaning?"

"I've been Guying it for more than a year now. The first year was all the same only getting more so. Now it's different."

The answer was a shock to Eileen. Apparently Guy had been the whole motif of the past fourteen months, not just an edging of embroidery.

"How, different?" she asked.

"Well, we could have talked together or walked together for ever, and we had an illusion we understood each other. Really! How should we? Well, it was very nice. It is very nice still. I don't think he's so fond of me when I'm not there, but when I am he is. I know him less well, and then sometimes we are even more intimate. There is less to say and he wants to kiss me."

A slow smile curved her mouth and she looked as though she tasted something sweet like honey. Eileen said bitterly:

"You gratify him, I'm sure."

"Oh I think he's quite gratified, yes," said Claudia pleasantly, "unless gratification implies an element of surprise."

A need to hurt Claudia came over Eileen. A possessive instinct to prove her strength. She felt that in her own happiness with Tommy she was isolated in a tower and losing her grip upon the rest of her life. She began smoothly, in her cool, attractive voice:

"He takes you for granted then?"

"It can't be helped," explained Claudia, "because I don't act to him. I should of course, but then I'm really fond of him."

"So you just serve yourself up on a dish. What will he think of you when you've trotted after him a little longer?"

"Worse than that! He won't think of me at all!"

"It's women like you who are really cheap. You might be better if you were a bad lot, a type complete in a way, vital, amusing. Fooling round with a few clandestine kisses, you're just innocent and vulgar."

Claudia was strangely unmoved. She said: "I know. But I think he doesn't know—yet."

"You couldn't be exciting. One could only love you for being white and fragrant. You're silly. You'll disgust him."

"No, he's too kind. I shall bore him."

"And when he's bored?"

"He must know by now in a way that I love him. When he's bored he'll—realise that I do. Do you see the difference? He'll resent me then because he'll feel a cad and yet know it was my own doing. Then he'll be very good and give me up and not let me sacrifice my time to him any more. And I shall think, 'He's tired or he's worried or he's feeling ill, I mustn't be touchy,' and go on ringing him up till the first year of our friendship is all blurred out and I'm a ridiculous nuisance but a nice little thing. Then I shall give it up and he'll forget."

In face of so much wisdom and such utter folly Eileen felt suddenly powerless. She came to her real grievance.

"But Claudia, how does he make you so happy; happy away from him even and everything; so happy in yourself; when now you know all that?"

She explained: "I know it but I don't believe it. I feel quite safe and the world's all right because it is still he who says when we part, 'When do I see you again?'"

For a moment Eileen was isolated again in her tower with her happiness and Tommy. How could he ever have ceased to ask her, "When do I see you again?" And what would it be like to be Claudia in six months' time? It could not have happened to Eileen so it was unimaginable. But formidable. Claudia could have no pride. It was not even as though Guy were dangerous and passionate. He held her accidentally with a little sentiment, a little charm. The thing was of her choosing, not his. He was quite simple; nice, selfish, responsive, pleasure-loving. Not in the least dangerous, just fatal for Claudia.

"Do you want to marry Guy?" asked Eileen.

"Of course not. How could I? What about Carol? Everything's all right how it is."

Eileen, a fighter herself, made a furious gesture. Claudia continued placidly:

"Several of his friends have thought it just worth while to say to him, 'You'll divorce Carol and marry that girl. I know you'll marry that girl,' so as to make quite sure he won't. But they really needn't have bothered."

"Claudia, you'd never—you'd never live with Guy?"

Claudia was completely surprised. "No, of course."

"Considering how you seem to feel I don't see your 'of course.'"

"You see," said Claudia, advancing the only sound reason that presented itself to her, "I don't think he'd be likely to want to." And she explained "After all when I'm a perfectly nice girl, and when I suppose he really could even get a divorce, and things are very pleasant how they are, and he's not very like that, I don't think either of us could. Do you?"

"I wish you'd pull yourself together, Claudia, and find a Tommy of your own."

"I wouldn't look as high as that!" she laughed.

"After all, there are so many fish in the sea. You must know that there are thousands of better and handsomer and cleverer men than Guy."

"Oh yes, I've noticed that myself."

"And people just as clever and amusing."

"Sure there are, darling! But they're not for me."

5

⬅ ➡

The amity, that wisdom knits not, folly may easily untie.

Troilus and Cressida, SHAKESPEARE.

Claudia dropped in on Guy at his house for nine o'clock breakfast one day. It was her only chance to see him before he went for a few days on business to Glasgow; a thing which men simply will do, in defiance of the advice of their female friends. They were quite used to breakfasting together thus. They kissed each other perfunctorily and settled down to eat, and to look at their letters, Claudia having brought her post along with her.

"What have you got, Claudia? Anything amusing?"

"Oh, just invitations and things."

"Pass them across and I'll see if you may accept them."

"Now then, Guy, I don't want any blasted sauce from you. What've you got yourself?"

"Just business and bills … oh no, here *is* something rather pure and fragrant! I've got an invitation to a debs' dance."

"You can't have."

"But I have. Look."

"Somebody must have borrowed an awfully old list."

"Don't be catty, child. It's simply that I'm getting into the right set at last. I'm going to have it framed and hung over the drawing-room mantelpiece."

He immersed himself in the paper. She got on with her breakfast, and getting up presently to pour herself out a second cup of coffee she saw that he was ready too and poured him out one at the same time.

"Thank you so much."

She wondered if perhaps she shouldn't have waited on him, but anyway it was too late now.

"Any news, Guy?"

"The Conservative won the Digglesbury by-election, just that touch of coral pink lends chic to a black straw, half a human face and two fingers have been found in a newspaper parcel in Shoreditch, and Mrs. Dogsbody Lane has had twins. Let me get on with the financial section now!"

There was silence for a little.

"There's the *Mail* and the *Express*," said Guy hospitably. "Do have a look at Beachcomber. I say, it's getting late and you've almost finished. I wish you'd read me the racing news while I lower my sausage."

"All right. How are things in the City?"

"Rotten."

"Here's the racing news. What do you want to know?"

"Oh, pass it to me, darling. … Thank you … Good Lord! Do you know that Derek Denzel had £40 on Burlington Bertie at eight to one? We must ring him up about this. I dined with them last night. They were in splendid form and bickered at the tops of their voices from caviare to Cointreau. Where were you last night, Claudia?"

"Quaglino's with Harold."

"Did you behave nicely?"

"That's nothing to you."

"I promise you it will be a lot to you if you didn't!"

"Not to be impertinent. Oh, Guy!"

"Yes?"

"Guy, in general theory, is it a good thing for girls to be hopelessly innocent like I am? I used to think they should be, but I don't know. P'raps it makes them rather asses."

"There," said Guy, "you've started a very difficult question. I think it is a good thing really. Only I must admit that all the little pieces who tell me things I'd meant not to learn for another ten years are certainly a great deal easier to talk to. You've not finished, have you? Let me get you an apple or something?"

"No thanks. Guy, do you think the Denzels are happy together?"

"You mean because they fight so much? Well, I think they like it. I should find it rather tiring, but Delia's got so much vitality and Derek isn't very sensitive. Not a delicately-strung couple! It's all quite friendly and they can't have any idea what it sounds like. It's certainly amusing! Would you like to help me choose a dressing-gown some time, Claudia?"

"Love to. Where shall we look?"

"I've seen one or two possibles in Jermyn Street. I'll look round."

"Blue do you think, Guy?"

"Blue, yes. Or brown with cream. Or white might be nice. Come along. You're walking me to my Underground, aren't you?"

"All right."

"I've got rather a tiresome board meeting this afternoon, and then off to Glasgow. What a life. Shall you write to me?"

"Do you want me to?"

"I think you'd better, to be on the safe side!"

"Did you happen to notice how the Craddock trial was going, Guy?"

"Didn't have time, you were talking so much! But he did it of course. Burke'll get him off though. Talking of the Denzels, would you like your husband to be as jealous as Derek?"

"Certainly not, except that anything's better than complete indifference."

"I believe you'd love it! You'd be so flattered."

"Rubbish. One doesn't want that sort of thing. One wants to be too

– 77 –

close for misunderstandings. To have quiet as well as excitement. To be really together; like two different gases fused into one new force."

"My dear, don't want that. People don't fuse. They try and try, but they're too different. They think they've succeeded and when they find later that they haven't they're angry with each other."

She looked sharply up at him, trouble and disquiet in her face. Because people did so desperately want to fuse. Were none of the couples around her really one? Were human beings as such condemned to be eternally cut off from each other, and yet to strive after fusion for ever in vain? How futile, how pathetic the necessity even to hold hands; to hold hands while the minds were encased in bright glass globes of their own individuality. Inevitable tragedy of passion and of love. …

"Would you have time to be very sweet and pay this bill for me, Claudia?" he asked. "Here's two pound ten."

"Sure darling," said Claudia, as they walked out into the morning.

6

And when you've finished the song you're through, That's why they call it, I love you.

Folly to be Wise.

It happened one autumn evening that Claudia, having dined *tête-à-tête* with Guy at his house, got up, perhaps a little undecidedly, to go. She was now twenty-four and a half and for more than eighteen months she had been infinitely, astonishingly happy. Not only when with him; he didn't make the bits between seem blank; he coloured everything. When she got up so uncertainly to go, and crossed the hearth to his armchair, saying:

"Get up and say good-bye!"

instead of getting up he said:

"You can't go yet!"

and took her two hands and pulled her down on to the arm of his chair and then on to his knees. And it was nicer to be there than anywhere in the world. They kissed each other, and hugged each other and kissed each other and they sat there all settled down and happy till suddenly the springs of the chair broke. They jumped up and there was the underneath of the chair all sagging down. It was so shymaking and absurd, she felt she must carry it off somehow, so she led him off to the opposite armchair. But the atmosphere was different somehow.

They were still enjoying themselves, kissing each other, and then he asked her to kiss him again and she said, meaning nothing:

"Surely I've kissed you enough to last you the rest of your life." And strangely enough, she had.

About two minutes later something seemed to snap. Something intangible; not the springs again. They both got up at once. He looked at her with a kind of abstract disgust she hoped never again to see on any face she cared for. She told him to call up a taxi and he went to the telephone without a word. He was very kind. He saw her home. He even held her hand, as though to reassure her that he was still there, because they were so very far apart. He said it was his fault that they had behaved so specially badly that evening and he was sorry. He even warned her against men. But really there was nothing to say. A voice inside her said almost aloud "There will never be anything to say again." He was very anxious on the doorstep that she shouldn't worry and should sleep. And, humouring him to the last, she slept quite well.

Claudia protracted the death agonies of the relationship as much as she could. She wrote him a four-page letter to say that everything was all right, and the past was over, and they'd be good and start all over again quite differently and easily and naturally, because dash it what friends they were. He sent a very sweet, brief answer to say he'd been feeling badly and yes they would start again. Next day they met by accident at a lunch party. It was unexpectedly jolly, and they walked together to his Underground station after, and it all seemed comfortable and ordinary and nice. She asked him to have her to lunch some time. She thought to herself it would be like the early days, as with any friend. She wanted to blot out the last *tête-à-tête*. He laughed and said maybe he would.

She thought he really would ring up and ask her to lunch. She had withdrawn so far already that she didn't see why he should be afraid of her trying to start it all up again. She hoped to see him from time to time like the rest of the world so as not to feel branded. She used to answer the telephone feeling almost sick, and all empty inside except for something plunging about. She had six weeks of it. She felt frightened at having the whole stream of that year's and last year's happiness dammed off so suddenly, not even a trickle left. All colour and all comfort gone. There was just her own voice saying, "I've kissed you enough to last you the rest of your life," and the secret voice in the taxi telling her, "There will never be anything to say again," and his blank, stranger face of nothing but disgust, and those broken, sagging springs.

After six weeks she ran into him in the street. It wasn't at all awkward. He got in the first attack by asking her why she never did anything about him now; then, which was nice and comforting of him, he said how pretty she was looking; then he explained, all serious and sweet, that he was being good about her and sacrificing himself and missing her frightfully. She just said: "Oh yeh?" a little derisively, and they smiled and passed on. The world did seem less hostile.

After they'd met she felt she couldn't bear another six weeks. She used to ring him up, and write, and make suggestions for meeting, and he always had most polite, convincing, regretful excuses. She used to think, "I mustn't be touchy. I hate difficult women who want to be exacting and make themselves felt instead of being natural." She must nearly have driven him mad, but all the same she didn't ask much. She really didn't want to own him or any part of his life, or land him with any responsibility for hers. She couldn't quite go on loving a man who was sick of the sight of her. But it seemed unfair, since he had forgotten that it had ever been nice, that he had ever felt soft towards her, that he wouldn't let her forget she'd made a fool of herself. Having loved him so much she hardly could forget him. He had been too important. Why shouldn't he make it easy for her by letting a new relationship take the old one's place? But what man ever believed a woman could stop adoring him? He felt tired and worried and a cad.

She ran him down at last. She was feeling rather gay and unemotional and pleased with life. She suddenly thought, "Its being over has at least the advantage that now we can occasionally be pleasant, useful companions and escorts for each other in the ordinary way." And then he let her have it all. He was a married man much older than she, they mustn't meet again, my dear, how good he was going to be about her (she quite expected to hear him say, "This hurts me more than it hurts you, my boy") and what a sacrifice it was and how it was all because he liked her so very, very much in a different way and was so *really* fond of her. There was nothing for it but another, "Oh, yeh?" and another smile.

7

J'en vais pleurer, moi, qui me laissais dire
Que mon sourire
Etait si doux.

Musset.

Sont elles assez loins, toutes ces allégresses,
Et toutes ces candeurs!

Verlaine.

Claudia Heseltine was not actually pretty. She had a very thin face, two profiles stuck together as they say, with a pointed nose and chin and permanently surprised eyebrows and an exceedingly sweet mouth. Her hair was in the half-grown stage, barbered into curls round the ears and nape. She had a good figure, looked effective and dressed well. She had chosen at the age of twenty-four to look smart rather than young. Very little of all this was apparent as she got off at the strange station and began looking for a strange chauffeur who might be looking for a strange guest, for a thick weight of fog lay over the Midlands. It was the first of January and the New Year had opened with complete darkness.

Claudia had been dancing the New Year in till four o'clock that morning. It had been a good party, noisy and vulgar but with an element of genuine gaiety. For the most part she had enjoyed the evening and from time to time she had dramatised her troubles and herself, dancing to forget. She had been the youngest person there. Sometimes she had chosen to think that she was also the unhappiest; sometimes she had leaned to the theory that under their masks they were all unhappy, making the best of a bad world, strangers dancing together to forget. Not such a bad way of forgetting, God help the dancers! It was fun dramatising things. Her mouth had twisted into laughter as men who didn't care for her began, as the evening latened, to think that perhaps they did. Lights and noise and movement and champagne and human companionship with its streak of casual, transient kindness, they made a good drug mixed together that both soothed and exhilarated. It all helped.

She thought, as the strange chauffeur tucked a fur rug round her in the strange car, that that party had been a swan song, a farewell to her old life with the old year. A good farewell, a good life, a good year until lately. She had had twenty-two years that hadn't been life at all, just preparation for the next two years of pleasure strangely ordinary and innocent to bring so much disaster. Now she had got to make a new life. She must. It had been a very fitting swan song. Everyone had been there except Guy himself, everyone at least of her older, livelier set. All the people who would never look at her without smiling and thinking of Guy, though they would see Guy night after night and not think of her.

Very, very slowly, the strange car carried her through the dense mass of fog towards the new life. The fog gave a strange effect of shutting away from her the old year, the past and the future. It was so enveloping, so isolating, and the car slurred on so slowly that time seemed to stand still while she set her house in order. She felt rather happy—she even felt that she had accepted this hunt ball invitation by divine providence and would meet her fate at the end of the drive. She did not think last year's troubles could follow her through such a weight and thickness of all-covering fog.

This time last year a whole orchestra had played in her heart. London had all gone colour of the rose, rabbits had gambolled about Piccadilly, lilacs had flowered out of manholes and violets along the pavement curbs. Guy had been so sweet and such fun early last year, and the year before last. Well, of course, she had been incredibly silly from first to last, and love that isn't mutual isn't love at all. It is worth nothing to anyone and is therefore worthless. One cannot possess what one doesn't want, and so though Guy couldn't help knowing about it her love had not so much been given to Guy as thrown down the drain. She had rather chased him, poor darling, and so meaninglessly too. Damn a woman who chased a man without even having a scheme. It had been rather an impossible position for Guy; the truth will broadcast itself; no doubt his friends had laughed at him and she was not dangerous enough to do him credit. She had only wanted to go on being friends, see him a little, but still she had scarcely been a friend of his choosing and he couldn't force himself to be a friend for ever, just to help her through life, if friendship were dead. So it had to be the way it was now. He had asked her to go to hell, charmingly, inoffensively, unmistakably, irrevocably. There was nothing to be done ever. He would never be sweet to her or give her fun any more, he would never find her sweet or funny again. Well, funny perhaps but not in quite the same way! Poor sweet, how she must have bored him at the end.

"Serve him right," smiled Claudia to herself, undisturbed by this mortifying and accurate vision.

She felt quite safe and happy. The car was taking her to a new life. The fog had shut out Guy. Just as he had shut her out for ever and ever more, with the old year.

8

← →

Who, now, when evening darkens the water and the stream
    is dull,
Slowly, in a delicate frock, with her leghorn hat in her hand,
At your side from under the golden osiers moves,
Faintly smiling, shattered by the charm of your voice?
There to-day, as in the days when I knew you well,
The willow sheds upon the stream its narrow leaves. ...
Who, now, under the yellow willows at the water's edge
Closes defeated lips upon the trivial word unspoken,
And lifts her soft eyes freighted with a heavy pledge
To your eyes empty of pledges, even of pledges broken?

                        EDNA ST. VINCENT MILLAY.

Claudia didn't meet her fate at the hunt ball, and the fog and the New Year did not shut Guy for ever out of her mind. But at first she thought both these had happened, so spirited a flirtation did she have with a very nice, pleasing young man; laughing with him and making eyes at him gaily of an evening and talking, beautifully and earnestly on barren hillsides during the day. When she got back to London she wanted never to see him again. But she wanted to have another similar young man. She provided herself with a succession of them, tiring of them too quickly to do them much harm.

She knew plenty of men who were real friends as well as plenty of women. Old childhood's playmates, ex-flames now married or well over any risk from her, and the happy, devoted husbands of women she was fond of, such as Tommy Reynolds and Noel Carstairs. But these did not suffice. She had acquired a taste for relationships at once more frivolous and more sentimental. More than a taste; what she called "that sort of thing" had become a habit and therefore in some sort a need. But she could no more go far with any of them than she could do without them altogether. As soon as a serious element came in, Guy would be too vividly presented to her by affinity or contrast. There would be neither heart nor spontaneity left.

At first the resilience of her spirits led her to suppose that she would get over Guy and marry soon. Dear Guy. It wasn't as if she loved him any more. She wanted to be friends with him for the sake of other days and accordingly resented his retirement into inaccessible mystery. But as to loving him, there could be no more question of that now that she recognised him as the stranger he had always been. Why she even knew him better. He would never surprise her now. In any case the Guy he had been when she had loved him didn't exist any more; the Guy she had thought him had never existed; the Guy she thought him now probably didn't exist either; while equally what she had been, what he had thought her and what she had thought herself, was gone for ever too. She had no hankering for his hand or his heart, since everything was changed in so many ways. Because it was changed she wanted the casual friendship of the new Guy to obliterate the old one. But she had only the old Guy, always lying in wait for her, always ready to pounce if she should try too hard to set up an interloper in his room. She had no idea of being faithful to ghosts, but she could not have managed to kiss one of his would-be successors. Some sudden vision of the past Guy would come out of the blue and oust the present from its place.

Claudia took very energetic measures about the haunting habits of the particularly silly past. She decided that the chief obstacle to human happiness was that its first necessities were irreconcilable opposites; to be free and not to be lonely. So far as anyone could combine these two ideals, she could; being so happily placed in her home life. She must take a lot of trouble about her friends and fill her life with independent interests and resources.

It was not in Claudia to go, as the females crossed in love sometimes do, to the good. She had to have her parties and her attractive, attracted young men. She had to be hospitable. She took much pride in her person so that she was well-dressed, well-barbered and well, if slightly, made up. She adored London. She was very gay-minded. She was always hoping to push off on to somebody else the slum visiting with which Rosemary Crane had landed her. She swore she would give it up every time she had to see Mrs. Scut of Limehouse, who had no roof to her mouth and yammered, surrounded by more smells than any even of her neighbours.

Equally of course Claudia couldn't go to the bad. Her ideas of self-respect were rather material: constant clean underclothes, two baths a day, creditable young men. Still, she was fastidious. And loving no man, she recovered something of her lost soul, the love of and wonder at beauty she had had at thirteen. She became far fonder of the country, and a little, but not very much, fonder of country life. She hunted more regularly in the winter, and bought a dog to comfort, she said, her childless middle age.

Happy in her home, happy in her friends, enjoying herself so easily in so many ways, Claudia could not see why she should not attain once more to actual happiness. But happiness cannot be dragged in from the outside. It is either there of its own accord inside you, or it is not. When it is there, outside things act as stimulants, releasing it in lovely bubbles within. If it is not there the outside things fill in the time and are as good a substitute as you can get. Claudia was her usual self, gay go up, gay go down, a little temperamental but not introspective, and having plenty of fun.

As time went on, still on occasions, when she was off her guard, pictures of Guy in the past would draw themselves sharply before her. The instant that she was tired or unhappy or ill and forgot to raise barriers against him, there he was. Guy singing to the banjo. Guy playing tennis, his open shirt revealing the set of his head and neck that she so loved. Guy wanting to give her a new coat, not because he was feeling attracted but because he hated his friends to be cold. Nothing is so poignant as the remembered kindness of those who have ceased to be kind. Claudia, tired or unhappy or ill, would want more than anyone in the world Guy to come and comfort her.

9

"Les deux grands secrets du bonheur, le plaisir et l'oubli."
"Et le chagrin?"
"C'est le penser—et c'est si facile de le perdre!"

La Nuit Venitienne, MUSSET.

When Claudia met Hugo again she was amazed to remember how little she had thought of him, how little she had reproached herself for what she had done to him. He looked more of a man now. Older and better able to cope with the world. He bore no malice for her abominable behaviour. Having avoided her all this while—it was nearly four years since they had met—now that he had found her again his old delight in her companionship revived. Claudia could not deny him her companionship, indeed she enjoyed his mind. But she learnt to understand the loathness of the once pursued to have any further dealings with the one-time pursuer. Not that Hugo was in the least pathetic or doglike. But there were ghosts between them. She had failed him too seriously. With him she felt, not resentment, not discomfort, but some mild shadow of both. She generally did her reluctant best for him, and when she wasn't very nice she told herself it was because if she were too nice he'd never marry. Ultimately the renewed friendship more or less lapsed and she was rather sorry.

Of course she took a great interest in Hugo's career. He was now quite a considerable popular novelist. She used to search his works as they came out for references to herself, and feel mingled relief and disappointment at finding none. Only one description of a girl struck her as, unintentionally, very apt for her. It said: "Phyllis thought in a cold, detached way that she would have made a good wife. She had almost everything. She was young, good-tempered, intelligent; she had good looks which she knew how to make the best of; she had capacity for enjoyment, a certain grace, a sufficient spark of humour; she had health and a little money. She was competent, companionable and kind. She had everything except—except panache. Except that touch of the radiant, the brilliant, the vivid that some so vitally possessed. Everything—except that the Thames would be safe from any firebrand she might carry ever."

Claudia took an even greater interest in Guy's career. She often heard of him from Carstairs, Denzels, Cazlitts, Alan Vane. She was always hearing of him. The world seemed littered with traces of Guy. Once he managed to persuade Carol to leave the stage again, and made great efforts to rebuild his marriage. But the reunion collapsed in due time. Claudia was glad, and wondered how she could reconcile her gladness with her constant statement to herself that his happiness was all she wanted.

When she was twenty-seven, nearing twenty-eight, she very nearly got engaged to Lord Santock. She was in great hopes, until he proposed, that he would do. He was well off, rather charming and amusing, presentable looking, well made, sufficiently in love with her, and rather good socially, which Claudia was enough of a snob for her age to mind about. He rode, danced, shot and played tennis well. She went so far as to tell her parents and the Reynolds and Alan Vane that she would marry him. But his proposal, a charming proposal, she found quite shattering. For there between them was Guy of nearly three years ago, asking for that kiss which lasted him the rest of his life. There between them was the six weeks when she had waited for Guy to ring her up, those lost, empty weeks, those ravaged six weeks. Feeling very guilty and ashamed she refused her lover and went back and cried bitterly from sheer disappointment.

But afterwards she was glad. It was nice to be your own woman. She loved her parents and Chesnor, she loved her friends and her own pursuits, she was a good daughter and a good friend and it was a grand world. Of course it was irritating the way people said of the most attractive single woman who had refused endless proposals: "And yet you'd have thought she'd have had chances, wouldn't you?" While the most stocky female who accepted the first offer that came her way was in the triumphant position of being a married woman. Still it would be some years before Claudia ceased to be able to reassure herself: "I could be married to-morrow if I wanted to." Freedom had its material compensations. And there were rather thrilling spiritual compensations in possessing your own soul.

One day soon after Claudia's twenty-eighth birthday she and Eileen were at the piano in the drawing-room of the flat, running through a large pile of old dance music such as many would have thrown away but such as they treasured. It covered a great range of years, and the various tunes could bring back astonishingly concrete impressions of past happenings and of dead thoughts. Besides, they were very good songs. Of such pawns of fashion as dance music, only the best survives the indifferent passage of time to flower again out of the arid past into the green present. The bad songs are all forgotten and lost, while this year's good ones are hedged about with the inevitable mediocrities. This is why we think old tunes are the best. Sometimes there is also sentiment; then perhaps they remind us so vividly of when the past was green that it is suddenly the present that seems arid.

To-day they leaned to mush. They sang "Lover, come back to me." They went further back and sang "It is lonely in Kalua now that you are not there." They went further back still and sang "You'll be sorry some day you left behind a broken doll." Then Claudia ran her fingers through her permanently waved curls and said:

"All these songs—could they help not sticking to those girls? How much nicer for the man too if the magic could have gone on for both of them. Nobody wants to get tired of the other person."

"Well," began Eileen in her cool, balancing voice, "sometimes the man's so weak that as soon as he's away from her he must experiment with some new feminine appeal, and then new claims arise. It's a failure of control. He can help that, or if he can't, he's not up to as much as a man who can. Then I think the moonlight-in-Kalua chap probably started all wrong, not thinking, meaning nothing, just feeling moonlight and love went well together and he must have someone. He would be to blame."

"I don't think it was like that," contended Claudia, almost seriously. "I think he thought here at last was a sweet little thing who could more or less hold him and whom he wanted for good. And she wasn't a woman who could hold him, and the magic died on him and he was disappointed. It was worse for her, but he wouldn't have stopped wanting what he had if he could have chosen."

"Whichever of them tires like that," Eileen admitted, "perhaps can't help tiring. If they're married, children or social considerations demand that they put their backs into it and try. If they're not, there's nothing on earth the one who tires can do, except walk out on it."

"Exactly," said Claudia. "After all, if you're not sure of a thing you must try it and see how it goes. If you both try it you both take a risk; either could have refused to play. The man in the song didn't want to break dolls. Baby dolls will go around being so brittle. How annoying of her first to cease to inspire or amuse him, and then to break. All the poetry he had once felt for her was wasted. Of course he found another one, but still he had a grievance against Fate too."

Eileen, patting down her smooth, trim golden hair with its wide water wave, asked: "Are you justifying your treatment of Hugo, or are you dramatising yourself and Guy? After all, he wasn't much of a past. I doubt if you figure in his past at all."

"Oh, I expect I annoyed him enough to be remembered when he reviews his whole past life in detail!" suggested Claudia smiling. Then she added: "You know, I can understand now his dropping me rather inconsiderately like a hot potato."

"Sick of the thought of you," explained Eileen helpfully. "After all, first you seemed so fragrant and different, and then, having probably prattled about wild flowers and preached about purity, you turned out to be a common, cuddly little thing, and yet you were still as ignorant and innocent as dammit, so what was the good of you? You were old enough to look after yourself, and you did rather hand yourself out on a silver salver."

Claudia burst into laughter. "Well, I do seem to have sown the wind and reaped the whirlwind!"

"That reminds me," said Eileen, "the Windhams' dance ..." And they discussed social engagements, men, clothes, housekeeping and Eileen's babies, until Eileen went.

Claudia sat on in the window seat. The March sunlight streamed into the pleasant room. It came in a flood of warmth and light upon her face. Daffodils lifted their golden trumpets as though ready to sound. The rust-red centres glowed in the moon-pale faces of the sweet, giant narcissi. In yet another vase, deep, burnished chestnut tulips stiffly upheld their chalices among the pastel green lances of their leaves. Outside, a barrel organ played the "Blue Danube."

Claudia was steeped in the gladness of the afternoon. The warm sunlight was so beautiful in itself; the lilting tune made it a moment of luxury. She knew herself to be infinitely happy.

When the barrel organ moved on and clouds for a little while trespassed over the sun, her mood of reaction was nothing very severe. She knew herself to be attractive and fortunate; she would probably always be well off; she had an infinity of interests and many friends, of whom Eileen and Tommy at any rate would never fail her. Still, she had missed a woman's best in life.

"Just by sheer bad luck," reflected Claudia. "I would have had the sweetest of men to love and be loved by always, an interesting, intellectual life, a house of my own, children to beguile and worry and fill my middle age, perfect happiness—if I hadn't just happened to go to Farling instead of Gloucestershire for a week-end five years ago. One can't help oneself, can one? It seems funny it should be just blind chance!"

The sun came out again. She stretched like a cat in the window seat, reached a narcissus from a vase, and began to repeat poetry to herself, smiling and looking out of the window.

PART IV

GOING STRAIGHT ON

← →

1

Ce qu'il vit ce jour là, il ne le revit jamais.

Anna Karénine.

Who knows not love from amity.

FRANCIS THOMPSON.

There was a fire in the room: very comforting and gay. In front of the fire was a low stool, behind that a deep, soft sofa. Against one wall were shelves of books; opposite, a writing-table framed by the dull peach-coloured curtains of the windows. The door opened, and as Claudia came with hurried steps into the fire's glow, two open letters in her hand, the telephone began ringing. She shut the door and turned up the lights.

She crossed to the writing-table, threw down the letters and lifted the telephone receiver.

"Hullo … yes of course it is, Lalage dear … yes, longing to meet him again and the dazzling actress … how sweet of you … oh dear, but I can't! Not the week-end after next. … I can't really, I'm going to Gloucestershire. … What fun the party sounds. … No, I really can't possibly … darling, I tell you I can't … Thousands of thanks and I wish I could. … Good-bye, see you soon, Lalage."

She sat down at the desk and wrote:

DARLING ROSEMARY,—How sweet of you and I'd have loved it! And

I wanted to meet Lionel Byng. But I can't possibly, I'm week-ending with the Lesters. Isn't it damnable? Ever so many thanks and I am sorry. Let's ring each other up on Monday.

Your loving

CLAUDIA.

The other letter had to be answered too. It was from Hugo. Certainly it was a tragedy that his invitation should clash with two such good alternatives, the one so tempting, the other unique. Still he expected her; she had practically promised to go; and she would be bound to enjoy herself enormously. A peaceful week-end in lovely country, rambling about talking with Hugo. It was hard to realise the possible serious implication of the visit.

The Lesters turned out to be a good deal older than the Heseltine parents. They were old fashioned and conventional and charitable and respected, and they were something of a cock and hen who had hatched out a duckling.

"I used to feel a little bitter," Hugo confided to Claudia, "because I got so much opposition and discouragement and nagging when I started writing as a career, such plaintive head-shaking, and not a comfortable word about it until I'd made good and they could be a little proud of me. But now I think they were quite right. A semi-literary, precious son who didn't make good would be an awful thing to have. Even successful novel-writing isn't really what I'd choose for my sons if I were likely to have any say. However, Mummy and Dad are delighted with me now, and they really are *such* dears. I do hope you'll like them."

Mr. Lester was square, and red faced, and white bearded, and he dressed in the rather loud tweeds and curious, shapeless, green hats that elderly county gentlemen sometimes affect. Mrs. Lester was faded, a little shrunken, with wispy grey hair and a face that would have been meek but for her piercing, beady eyes. She dressed in nondescript black, more or less as Mrs. Noah. She kept abreast of all modern movements and developments by careful study of intelligent magazines, journals and reviews. They were both intensely religious. Mr. Lester was a churchwarden, read the lessons and passed the plate. Claudia did not quite know why she found this oppressive, for she was after all a reasonably frequent churchgoer, her parents were very genuine Christians and her father even read the lessons himself. Here, however, it was all rather heavy and funereal. She did actually like her host and hostess but they made her nervous, she felt that she would make floaters and they would not like her. They were certainly kind. Mrs. Lester kissed her, and fussed over her comfort. Mr. Lester talked loudly and painstakingly on simple, trivial subjects which might be supposed to be within the grasp of her frivolous mind.

One comfort was that it was a perfectly lovely house. It had been built in the early seventeenth century of the warm, grey local stone. Some day someone would have to overhaul the hot water apparatus and install more bathrooms, but still it was comfortable. It was not furnished with faultless taste, but it contained that not too crowded jumble of its good things with time honoured rubbish that makes a place very undeniably a home. Around the house was much turf, some good trees, rose bushes run rather wild about a sundial, and a formal garden with clipped yews and boxes, a fountain and pavemented walks. At the drive gates rambled an adorable stone village; warm grey cottages with vivid gardens, grouped about winding, rutted, uneven roads, and exquisite grey stone bridges over the wide stream that bounded the garden of the big house on one side with its eternal rustle and swish. All around were great spaces of fields, separated by little walls and never a hedge, climbing away to a wooded horizon.

The household went early to bed. After Mrs. Lester had left Claudia in her room, Hugo crept in to see that she was happy and comfortable and to say good night.

"How are you liking it?"

"It's lovely, Hugo. It's a heavenly place. And your mother and father are so nice to me; they're dears, aren't they?"

"Oh Claudia, I *am* sorry I didn't warn you we'd got such a bad cook!"

She laughed. "Don't be silly, Hugo. She isn't all that bad. Anyhow, it's nice to have plain things. You didn't tell me anything about it at all! You didn't tell me I'd have such a marvellous romantic room. Not haunted, I hope, is it?"

"No. I'm so glad you like it. The tapestry chair covers are rather good. Unlike the ancestors in oils!"

She looked at the old mirror over the mantelpiece, the dark, rather wavering picture it reflected framed in dull, carven gold.

"Don't you love old looking-glasses?" she said dreamily. "They always thrill me. I like to think of your lost, dead ancestresses, young and supple, with beautiful rose petal skins; all their secrets and their wild, young thoughts hidden such a little way behind their shining, inscrutable eyes. I can see them looking deep into the mirror, combing out their long, heavy hair all in the soft glow of candlelight.

> And I lack the heart to scold.
> Dear, dead women—with such hair too!
> What's become of all the gold? ..."

"Claudia dear, I'm afraid you'll be bitterly disappointed by the family history if you've made up your mind that all my ancestresses were beautiful wantons!"

She began to laugh. "What a horrid wet blanket you are."

It was on the third and last evening of the visit, after Sunday supper, that Hugo proposed. It was a warm night for February, almost as mild as summer, and there was a golden crescent moon and a dusting of stars.

"Come out for a little, Claudia," said Hugo. "It's too lovely to stay indoors."

"I'd like to come."

The eyes of the older Lesters met with an almost audible click. Pointedly they sighed. Claudia and Hugo left very demurely, but once out of earshot they broke into a run and giggled loudly from reaction and relief. They were in day clothes (the Lesters did not dress on Sunday night) and she had caught up a little scarlet jacket before going out. But they did not feel so very warm after all. A sudden solemnity came upon them; they walked down the drive into the village and across a bridge to a wide, sodden field, shivering slightly, in complete silence. They turned back and looked at the house and the cottages and the church, cleanly carved out of the shadows. A sudden violent shivering came over Hugo.

"You're cold, Hugo?"

"No. Are you?"

"Not very."

"I love you, Claudia. Do you mind?"

"N-no."

"Are you fond of me at all? You are a little fond of me, aren't you?"

"Yes."

"Please, please marry me, Claudia. Will you marry me, darling?"

"Yes, if you want."

Her voice was almost a whisper, a very little voice, but hardly hesitant. She must give him what he asked, he was so dear a friend. She leant against him in his arms and they stood linked in their first kiss, her scarlet jacket showing up in the yellow moon, plain for any passer by to see. He held her close after they had kissed, and she stared over his shoulder, wonderingly up the dark field to the thin crescent and the stars, trying a little desperately to realise that she was engaged and belonged in a new mysterious way to Hugo. Now he wanted to kiss her again, but she didn't much mind, and it was nice when he was stroking her hair.

"Darling, darling sweetheart," he said. "I can't believe it, it's so wonderful. I'm so happy I want to write something gigantic and make you proud of me. You're so beautiful."

"I am proud of you, darling. I hope I will make you happy. You're so good."

"Beloved, I'm almost too happy. Are you happy? Are you?"

"Ever so happy, sweet. But I feel shy."

"Do you love me a little? I love you so much, please say you love me."

"I love you," said Claudia gently, staring away at the moon.

2

←→

For, thogh that wyves been ful holy thinges,
They moste take in pacience at night
Swich maner necessaries as been plesinges
To folk that hav y-wedded them with rings,
And leye a lyte hir holinesse asyde
As for the tyme; it may no bet betyde.
The Man of Law's Tale, CHAUCER.

It was great fun talking about the engagement. Claudia had endless
lovely girlish chats with her mother and Eileen. Everyone was pleased
about it. Even Mr. and Mrs. Lester, having decided to make the best of
her, discovered that she had some serious tastes and was certainly nice
mannered and attentive. She would let their son lead his own life, they
felt, and on her next visit to Gloucestershire they got quite fond of her
pretty presence and her gaiety. Mr. Lester was even found to respond to
mild teasing.

The engagement was as happy as such an exhaustingly busy period
can be. Mr. and Mrs. Heseltine were pleasantly, easily sympathetic;
Eileen and Hugo were becoming fast and intimate friends; Hugo was
radiantly in love; and Claudia had no ghastly tremors and doubts. He
was so gentle with her and yet so happy and assured; she loved his
endless flow of high spirits and talk, and thought him the sweetest, most
companionable person in the world. The evening before her wedding

she found that her mother contemplated telling her various things of vaguely sinister import. But she was tired and nervy and wanted to go quickly to bed, to forget everything in dreamless sleep, to be fresh and looking her best in the morning. Besides it was all inevitable now; and anyway marriage was the usual lot of woman. So she stopped her mother by pretending that she knew everything already.

Claudia and Hugo had a fashionable London wedding. She wore a long, slim dress of white panne velvet with a sheath of white lilac and a light, frothy lace train. The bridesmaids wore a deep, warm tone of rose, and held before them bunches of shaded tulips. As Claudia and Hugo signed the register the voices of boys sang crystal clear and void of all emotion, "Love one another with a pure heart, fervently: see that ye love one another." Eileen smiled at Tommy and thought that those were indeed the two requisites of love. "With a pure heart, fervently." Not one without the other. Not either, but both. "*See* that ye *love* one an-*oth*-er. See that ye love one anoth-er."

Claudia cried a good deal on her honeymoon. Hugo was very understanding and forbearing and kind. They had many tastes in common, and she did manage to enjoy a certain amount of the thing. Even honeymoons have their lovely interludes, and improve with time and patience as they proceed.

3

← →

Délie elle-même à son tour
S'en va dans la nuit éternelle,
En oubliant qu'elle fut belle,
Et qu'elle a vécu pour l'amour.
VOLTAIRE.

Literature of course is not the ideal trade for a husband. Instead of pushing him off to the office from half-past nine till six, the wife has him about the house all day. And his work does not end at six. He may want to write till bedtime and even after. His work made Hugo exceedingly inhospitable. Sometimes he felt sociable and liked to go out (though not of course to dances) and see friends, but he generally hated them to be asked to the house because of the erratic movements of his inspiration— with the exception, that is, of occasional editors and literary men. If he were the visitor he could leave when the spirit moved; he could not kick other visitors out when he wished.

"But darling, if I have them in a different room you needn't see them,"

"Yes, but you know that always makes me want to see them!"

Claudia was quite good and cheerful about all this. After all, she had known beforehand that her young man was an author and had married him just the same! Her parents' flat was generally at her disposal; they were seldom there and she had a latchkey still. She joined two clubs, a comfortable, commodious day one and an uncomfortable, crowded day and night one, and did much entertaining at these. She was given to hospitality; but she was not unduly extravagant, and in spite of a taste for gaiety and clothes she made money go a long way. She never accepted anything for the two of them without consulting his wishes first. Occasionally she went dancing without him, that he might not think he must either come or else deny her a pleasure (and also because she wanted to). But she deserted him so seldom that he could not feel she had a side of her life apart from him.

Claudia and Hugo were exceedingly confidential and interested in each other's doings. The most trivial episodes provided thrilling matter to discuss. If sometimes the poor girl was completely widowed by his passion for work, she was thrilled by the results of the work after, and there were times when he slackened off his feverish activity and they dashed to the country, or wandered round London shops, or made sight-seeing expeditions, or had brief, radiant honeymoons abroad, very, very much happier than the first one. Hugo was sweet about being interested even in Claudia's most domestic thrills, such as the housemaid's fine, upstanding young man and the kitchen maid's prize at the parish hall fancy dress dance. And much as he abhorred the entire Carstairs set, he was fond of Rosemary Crane and Co., and simply bosom friends with Eileen and Tommy.

Marriage, Claudia decided, was an exceedingly pleasant state. Your work was clear before you, your problems were settled, your life was full, your husband was a friend of the closest intimacy and, if you were lucky, as nice to run about and do things with as a girl. You had an infinity of private jokes, so that it was fun to meet again even after two or three hours' absence.

Hugo, apart from abstraction and moroseness occasioned by his absorbing work, was completely radiant. It is sad to think of that ambitious stylist being involved in such a conversation as:

"Is the small thing a tired, sleepy one then? Did it think its little boy loved his pens and papers best?"

"Yes, howwid old pens and papers. Little boy thwow them away and come bye bye to please his Teddy bear."

Perhaps these things should not have been written down in cold blood. After all, they were but occasional.

By the end of three years there was only one slight anxiety: the continued nonappearance of the baby desired by both.

Hugo seemed to get no older during those three years. His boyishness was very nice in some ways, but as Claudia acquired increased confidence, beauty, poise, he did not move to match. He had greater common sense over theories; far more clear, decisive views; but in everyday life she was much the more competent, and more than her fair share, particularly over money matters, was left to her judgment. Occasionally he would dig his toes in, as when he chose Kensington and rejected Mayfair. But it was idle to appeal to him about gas, electricity, precedence at dinner, first mortgages, insurance, the motor-car, or wine.

Claudia could not always forecast her husband's reactions. Towards the end of their first year of marriage she heard of the sudden death in the street of an old flowerwoman she had sometimes dealt with. She perfectly remembered the old hag with her husky voice and breath that smelt of whisky. And now the papers had discovered on her death that she had once been Lou Delane, a queen of the music-hall stage, beloved in London, Paris and New York. It seemed very pitiful to Claudia to think of her ravaged beauty and her lost lovers and the rings that had gone to the pawnbroker long ago. And she hastened home to Hugo, wanting to hear him recite her lovely poems about death.

> We are such stuff as dreams are made on,

and

> Fear no more the heat of the sun
> And the furious winter's rages,

and coming to more modern times:

> Crimson and black on the sky, a waggon of clover
> Slowly goes rumbling, over the white chalk road;
> And I lie in the golden grass there, wondering why
> So little a thing
> As the jingle and ring of the harness,
> The hot creak of leather,
> The peace of the plodding,
> Should suddenly, stabbingly make it
> Dreadful to die.

Or perhaps

> How strange a thing is death, bringing to his knees,
>   bringing to his antlers
> The buck in the snow.
> How strange a thing—a mile away by now it may be,
> Under the heavy hemlocks that as the moments pass
> Shift their loads a little, letting fall a feather of snow—
> Life, looking out attentive from the eyes of the doe.

When she presented her case to Hugo he pointed out that all her sorrow and sympathy was entirely based on the fact that the deceased had not been an honest, decent working woman at all, but a tart. In this, apparently, lay the great pathos of the situation.

But Hugo could be very, very sympathetic. He was adorable about an illness of Eileen's the year after, and even one of the kitchen cat's the year after that.

4

← →

Blessed are the pure in heart, for they have so much more to talk about.

The Children, EDITH WHARTON.

Claudia's attention was apt to wander when Hugo held forth on politics over breakfast. But he was always very firm with her about it.

"Have you no patriotism, Claudia? One would think you didn't care about your country at all."

"But I'm a mass of patriotism. I'm all for the King, God bless him and my country, right or wrong. And I wish there were something like taking off their hats for women to do for the colours. And nothing on earth excites me like a military band. I never hear its rhythm and clash without a great surge of public school emotions. I want, if it could be done painlessly and without inconvenience, to die for a cause. Almost any cause!"

"*Really!*" cried Hugo with unutterable contempt. "Vamped up emotions like that aren't real at all. Pass the butter."

"They're as real as anything else," she maintained placidly. "Here's the butter. After all, there all those emotions are, sleeping in almost everyone, ready to flare into life for a military band. Just as surely as some cinemas or plays work you up to think of love; as certain types of music make you think restlessly of the faun following the nymph that flees in panic and yet wants to be caught. Sacrifice and selflessness and similar slop are just as existent, as real, as desire and all the things that nowadays are regarded as particularly solid facts."

"Oh yes. And they're so useful if they fade with the music, cut off by the space widening between you and the band."

"What do you want me to do, my sweet? Speak in Hyde Park? But seriously and leaving me out of it, is there much now that one man could do to help? Could another Pitt, for instance, do much to change things alone by his own powers? Short of a Pitt, what can one individual do?"

"I wonder. I believe one man who had real conviction and eloquence could do a tremendous amount by speaking all over the country, starting a movement, rousing people, inspiring them, waking them up. Oh, I would like to be that man! As it is, I don't suppose this will make any difference to a soul, but I've got a tremendous lot I want to say in my novels. Serious stuff I mean. Well, you've seen précis of ideas tabloided in the famous note-book! Darling, do you think my tripe will suffer if I start writing it with a purpose? It ought really to be all art for art's sake, oughtn't it?"

Claudia took a second roll thoughtfully. "I don't think I quite see the difference," she said. "Art's got to say something, hasn't it? And if humanity or your country is a passion with you and stuff about it *will* come out, why should it be less the genuine inspiration of your creative whatnot than if you wrote about decadence, or disillusion, or God, or love, or peasants in Siberia?"

"Oh, but proselytising stuff? Always bad, don't you think? At least it's dangerous. You wrest everything round to your moral with elaborate machinery and the story becomes contrived instead of being inevitable."

"Not if you keep a stern eye on your artistic conscience. 'How shall they hear without a preacher?' Preach, my sweet. Dash it, your books are read."

Hugo laughed. "So far, Beautiful. But will they be when I get into my nice new pulpit?"

"New?" crooned Claudia, "My darling love, the world is your pulpit."

"A high-minded fellow of Kensington," Hugo began, "took up a most moral and cleansing tone. How does it go on?"

She suggested:

> "His wife said, 'It don't hurt
> To make pies in the dirt,'
> So he …

Bother! I wanted to bring benzine into the rhyme because you could clean someone with it, but it won't do."

"Or do you think she said:

> 'It don't hurt
> To sling muck with a squirt'?"

wondered Hugo. "Anyhow, I'm afraid it can't be finished. At least not unless we weakly bring Kensington back into the last line. In which case he could bury or scrub her according to preference. Not very good, I'm afraid."

"Returning to the country," said Claudia, "I'm always sick with terror about some future war. And what I'm wondering is whether all that cant about its being harder for those left agonising behind, and they also serve who only stand and wait, has anything in it. Wouldn't women be compensated then for being under-dogs in the world, unimportant, inferior animals? Wouldn't they be lucky, lucky, lucky, to stay behind and escape the mud and the cold and the mud and the lice and the endless noise and the mud and danger and horror and death and pain and mud? Would I really give my soul to go too and face it all in action and drink of the cup you drank of? Or would I, if I were honest with myself, be thankful for once, at last, that I hadn't been born a man?"

But he ignored the main issue. He said mockingly, lovingly, "Inferior animal, do you really want to be a man?"

There was a silence. She busied herself with coffee.

"What are you smiling at, Claudia?"

"Oh, I don't know."

"A penny for your thoughts."

"All right. As long as you pay up. I was thinking, oh, that it used to be rather fun with Harry and Clive, and how much more fun it would have been if I'd been as old as I am now."

"In fact what fun you could have now with another Harry or Clive?"

"Not to laugh at me," said Claudia with dignity, and he held out his hand for hers and gave it a squeeze.

5

← →

(*Inscription pour une statue de l'Amour*)
Qui que tu sois, voici ton maître;
Il l'est, le fut, ou le doit être.

VOLTAIRE.

Hugo allowed Claudia to accept the Carstairs' dance for them both, because all her friends would be there, because even he would enjoy the cabaret, because she had bought a new frock; but on condition that they dined quietly at home. When the evening came, genius was burning luminously. They dined together unchanged, he because he had worked till the gong went, she because she thought it would be vaguely matier to dress afterwards too.

"I wish I weren't still in such a good vein," grumbled Hugo. "It's tired me out already so that I'd like to go straight to bed. But I think I shall have to sit up for hours finishing the section."

"Oh darling! What about the dance?"

"I know, darling. I'm awfully sorry. I hadn't forgotten. But I really can't cope."

"But Hugo, you promised! I did want you to come to this and you never do."

"But you must be reasonable. Even if my writing isn't our bread and butter it's certainly the jam and the jelly and the marmalade."

"But just this one evening, Hugo."

"What can I do, Beautiful? I can't help the fit taking me to-night. You know I'd be a fish out of water. You wouldn't really want me at it."

"It's only just to arrive with me and dance one dance with me in my new dress, and I promise if you'll just keep me in countenance for the first plunge I'll float off on my own and you shall return in peace."

"But it isn't worth it to dress just to take you to the thing. And I shall meet people I know who'll expect me to dance with them. And I'm tired with this rush of words to the pen already, and it's all going round and round in my mind incessantly. Really, darling, you can go alone."

"But it's such an enormous, ambitious dance. I don't want to go alone!"

There was a raised, exasperated note in each of their voices. Neither seemed able to conclude the argument. He sat down hesitantly at his desk. She pretended to titivate a bowl of flowers. Then she quietly left the room.

Hugo was writing furiously when some time later his wife returned, discreetly scented and decorated, an elegant coat over her beautifully cut dress. She came up behind him, clasped her arms lightly round his neck and kissed the top of his head.

"Good night, darling. I'm vewwy sowwy I was such a silly, selfish Teddy bear. Of course work is not to be bothered and interrupted, and anyway, I oughtn't to take you when you're tired. I do hope you won't have to sit up terrible awful late. Tabloid what you can, won't you, into the note-book for to-morrow, and go to bed as soon as you can bear to stop."

"Sweetheart," said Hugo, feeling, perhaps undeservedly, a little ashamed of himself, "what an angel you are. I am a beast. Don't you really mind?"

"Ho, no, Mister, I don't mind. Husbands is terrible awful in the way, the other girls tell me." And she ran quickly to her taxi downstairs.

But she did mind. She knew the symptoms. She would be a widow now for weeks. That baby that wouldn't come ... She had wanted it first to do her duty and to please Hugo; now she wanted it for its own sake or hers. It was nice that they were week-ending at Chesnor; Hugo could work undisturbed and she could bully her parents for constant attention. And to-morrow was Eileen's nurse's half-day off and she would help Eileen pram-push in the park. Still she felt disconsolate and lonely, almost shy, as she ascended the front stairs of Lalage's house. Even though she managed to hide her feelings and swept on as though she considered herself Helen of Troy.

Looking round the landing after greeting her host and hostess, her eyes immediately fell upon a familiar face. She smiled her ready, delighted smile before she realised that it was Guy Verney, that she had seen him last three years ago when he had danced with her once, and that it was hardly credible that he could remember her. But he did remember.

Guy Verney could not have imagined beforehand that, at a ball where he knew and liked so many people, nay, at any ball whatever, he would have asked a woman he had only met once for a short while three years ago to dance with him. But she was looking lovely. There had been welcome in her recognising smile. They did remember each other quite well. He had been cut for the dance in progress by a tiresome little creature who liked to flirt more than he cared to. The said tiresome little creature had led two cavaliers to the ball, himself being one, and she wanted to play them off against each other. Guy's rival liked her well enough, but he himself was bored. The arrival without an escort of this charming Mrs. Lester was very opportune.

They knew a little about each other from the *Sketch*, the *Tatler*, and Mr. Charles Graves his column. He remembered pictures of her wedding and had read some of Hugo's books. She had seen his wife on the stage, had admired her, and speculated idly on the cat and dog life they led. They had little jokes about Noel and Lalage with which to break the ice.

They danced well and they fitted marvellously together. During her first dance with him other people came up to arrange various numbers with her, and at the end of it they parted with no plans to meet again. She felt a touch of chagrin, of disappointment, almost of resentment. Surely he must have enjoyed it as much as she had? But two dances later she encountered him again upon the stairs.

"Please can I have the next dance, Mrs. Lester?"

"Not the next, I'm afraid. I'm dancing it. What about number ten?"

They reached the landing, the doorway, the edge of the dancing floor.

"There's my partner looking for me and I'm sure that's yours. Come along quick!" urged Guy.

Without giving any consent she found herself dancing with him again.

Enchanted dance, enchanted floor, enchanted band! He held her close and she sang up at him, teaching him the words of the tune:

> "I've never been in love,
> But I want to be in love,
> Wonder, could I fall in love
> With you?
> Would you be mean in love,
> Twixt and between in love,
> Are your sex all in love
> Untrue?
> You are so sweet—I've never felt like this till now—
> But you're so sweet I've got to take my toss—and how!
> I've never been in love—
> Now I've got to fall in love.
> Honey, I'm all in love
> With you!"

This banal twaddle with its lilting, caressing tune, sounded infinitely disturbing crooned lightly, softly, in her clear, high-pitched voice. She looked up at him, half-laughing, teaching him the words which no one could be long in mastering. He held her closer; they danced beautifully; she was all light and relaxed in his arms; presently she shut her eyes and he took up the tune and the singing:

> "Wonder, could I fall in love
> With you?"

He was cold and unsusceptible, friendly but aloof, an intriguing problem to woman: yet not only could he, he actually did.

They sat out on a far-off sofa while all the company gathered to enjoy and applaud the cabaret. What they saw in each other no one can tell. There were many lovelier women in that house than Claudia—indeed she was not really lovely at all for all her airs of loveliness. There were lovelier, cleverer, more conspicuous and better women in that house than Claudia. And as to him, he was not good-looking at all, except in so far as a well-made man of six feet two may generally pass for handsome. He was ordinariness personified. He was perceptive but not penetrating, charitable but not unselfish, quick but not deep. He had a thin, sallow face, dark hair and moustache and protruding front teeth. He had a quiet way, a charming voice, a sincere manner and cynical eyes. Most people liked him. Why not? And then again, why did they? Claudia's eyes lost themselves in his, no longer cynical but very, very serious. Her fingers played with a spray of syringa. The heavy sweet scent of the light white flower hung between them like a prayer.

They were together all evening. When at the end of the dance he saw her home in a taximeter cab, she knew that something had happened to her that had never happened to her before, and that she must not see him again. And as he eagerly tried to make plans for their next meeting, she made her halting excuses; they didn't entertain, she never went out without her husband and he hated going out at all, oh just to-night it was because of Lalage and he'd had a headache. ... They drew up at her front door and the taximan waited while they argued till at last silence fell upon them, and still she could not summon the final resolution to go in. The taximan waited with little surprise; he was used to such delaying. Guy, staring at Claudia and feeling bewildered and hurt, saw suddenly on her face the blurred indecisive look of someone who would fain cry. Her mouth quivered and her eyelashes were shining and wet. He understood and couldn't bear it.

"Is it not that you don't want to see me again, but that you know I want to see you too much? Do you feel the same way? Can't we see each other any more?"

They confessed to each other, and then, feeling all exalted and pure and sentimental and noble and brave, they gave each other up for ever in the taximeter cab, and he saw her in.

6

⬅ ➡

Because women can do nothing but love they have given it a ridiculous importance. ... Men keep their various activities in various compartments and they can pursue one to the temporary exclusion of the other ... it irks them if one encroaches on the other. ... As lovers, the difference between men and women is that women can love all day long, but men only at times.

SOMERSET MAUGHAM.

The following morning Claudia awoke to the thought of Guy Verney. At first she lay hardly detached from the mists of sleep, and little sensations of pleasure flowered everywhere inside her. Then as she wakened wholly to the knowledge of their parting she felt that their meeting must have been a dream: an episode apart; something that, having taken so short a space of time, could not really matter as it seemed to matter. As the day went on she learnt that this was a vain hope. The reality of it lay upon her like frost.

Having found that it did indeed matter to her, she could not help wondering if it really mattered to him. Perhaps he had slept it off. Might he not have been glad of any semi-romantic interlude to pass an evening that might else have hung heavy on his hands? Just one evening? However genuine his emotion of the night, it might well seem very remote, very fantastic in the morning. But indeed she need not have worried, it was not so. Guy was in love for the fourth or perhaps the first time. The other three episodes, his calf love, his suitable engagement, his unsuitable marriage, had all produced some charming sensations. But this was different, not only in kind, as are they all, but in importance. It was the love of his life.

They had renounced each other in good faith. It was harder for Guy in two ways, namely that his love was the greater, and that his home life was unhappy and sordid. But in every other way it was easier for him, simply because he was a man. He had so many other interests, his successful business in the City, his prowess at the usual sports, a host of friends whom his independent habits allowed him to see all he would of. Any of these interests could occupy his mind completely for the moment. He did not think of Claudia when trunk calling Germany, or enjoying a good run, or entertaining a delighted gathering by singing naughty songs rather nicely to the banjo with a sufficiently demure, unconscious air. He thought of her fervently none the less. She was the point to which all his thoughts returned. They could be distracted from her very completely, but as soon as the interruption was over, around her image they naturally returned to rest. He might not always remember to want her when he was with others; when he was alone she was the one person he wanted every time.

But for Claudia there was no complete escaping from the memory of Guy. All day long behind the housekeeping books, the tailor's fitting, the cocktail party, Hugo's short story, there was the echo of his charming voice, the illusion of his troubled smile. She fought against it with much activity, but perhaps she did not honestly want to let it go. It was so thrilling, so lovely, so important. It was an awakening, a quite new breath of life. She was in all truth desperately unhappy over the hopelessness and the renunciation, but her natural energy carried her along and her sentimentality consoled her much with its rosemary and pansy wreaths of romance. Only always, always, through letter writing or argument or laughter she was faintly conscious of wanting Guy, of missing Guy, of loving Guy.

Claudia in her grief turned instinctively to Hugo and she found him an elusive and wobbly reed. She concealed her trouble well enough, he was not aware of a change in her, but perhaps it is unlikely that his making a discovery at this time was wholly coincidence. His discovery was that she did not love him and had never loved him. In this new knowledge he was well ahead of her. Even now she told herself that she loved them both, that she loved them differently, that she loved Hugo and was in love with Guy. Hugo, knowing nothing about Guy, yet felt betrayed. He could not blame himself, he had not lost her love, for now he saw that he had never had it. He had not asked to marry her upon those terms, he had demanded more than her hand, and she had deceived herself and him.

He could not do anything about it because so far as he knew nothing was changed. Things were so unchanged that he could not help often losing sight of the fly in his jam. A tremendous chasm had opened between them, but there they were, close together, she very sweet, and affectionately disposed towards him, he in love with her. Still he knew that she would never love him now in return as she should. He found this a lightness and a lack in her, and resented it in a way peculiar to himself. He was not passionate or masterful in love, but he had a rarefied ethical standard. Claudia had failed him, and was his true love no more.

Consequently he failed Claudia. Though they could not but be friends, talk eagerly, discuss his works, make their private allusions and jokes, tell each other their doings, any airs of flirtation or coquettishness or cajolery that she put on for him irritated him fiercely, the more so that he felt their charm. He developed a slight inclination to snub her and snap at her; at any rate he was somehow withdrawn from her. Being still unchanged towards him, she was hurt.

Hugo of course was far more deeply hurt. But he had a consolation denied to most of the world. How happy is the novelist, for every misfortune that befalls him is so much copy. His troubles are not only pounds, shillings and pence to him, but they may be praise and glory. The specialist's interest he must take in them must make them better worth while, and the unloading of them on to pages of paper does much to draw their sting. The story Hugo forthwith wrote was of a dissipated young man who proposed to a girl of seventeen for her money, who in her turn was shoved by her parents, ignorant as she was of life and love, into accepting him for his title, and who subsequently aroused in him an unexpected, true and purifying love to which she could never find in herself the slightest response. The emotions of the poor dissipated young man were not even wholly Hugo's emotions, but discoursing about them did him a power of good. As usual he required Claudia's opinion and interest, and she gave him some rather helpful advice about the triangular dénouement.

Guy was devoured by a deep and jealous love. Hugo was disillusioned and embittered for ever to his soul. But they slept little the worse. Dark shadows drew themselves round Claudia's eyes and she started at sudden sounds.

7

A vivre ton regard m'invite,
Il me consolerait mourant.
J'en vais pourtant, ma petite,
Bien loin, bien vite,
Tout en pleurant.

MUSSET.

It was true, true beyond a doubt, tragically true that the world of
love and virtue and wisdom was the true world.

THORNTON WILDER.

Things went much better in the house in Kensington when the
separation of Guy and Claudia came to an end. For it did come to an
end, chiefly by the kindness of the entire Carstairs set who, having seen
them at the Carstairs' ball, lost no opportunity of obligingly throwing
them together. The thing was in the air now, however careful the two
principals might henceforward be.

In furthering the affair these friends were not actuated by love of
scandal so much as by idle curiosity, nor by idle curiosity so much as by
genuine good nature. Guy the elusive, the intriguing, the circumspect
was vanquished at last. Claudia was charming and deserved her little bit
of fun. A decorative couple, good value, both dears.

Claudia and Guy began again at a much lower pitch and embarked on a platonic friendship. They meant to be in every way self-controlled, and they found much harmless pleasure in meeting often and doing things together. Claudia had him constantly to her house and the general atmosphere became more cheerful. Claudia and Guy were happy and her nerves calmed. Hugo despised Claudia for needing a tame cat and general escort, and this made him feel superior to her, and this again made him more friendly and unbending. Then he liked Guy who could talk easily and amusingly, and he did not despise him. Indeed, though Hugo was better and far cleverer, still the older man, the man of the world, the man who had been through the war, did have more presence. Moreover Hugo regarded Guy as useful copy for the average man.

Guy and Claudia began slowly enough. They met every week, and in spite of all their repressions there was something very natural and pleasant about their imitation friendship. But Eileen condemned it utterly from the start. She and Hugo discussed it freely together. Claudia found a tiny feeling of soreness at their ever increasing intimacy. Never very possessive, she yet felt a faint jealousy not for Hugo's sake but for Eileen's. The uncertainty of Eileen's alliance threw her more and more confidentially upon Guy.

Claudia and Hugo had only one row together. One evening she and Guy were alone and something he said reminded her of an idea in Hugo's note-book. She fetched it to show him, and they turned the leaves and looked at several passages, some quite in full, some abbreviated; all disconnected.

"This is so like me," said Claudia, and they read:

It would be quite easy if she pulled herself together and dealt with it. But somehow she could not take the simplest step. She was like someone lying in a hot bath and saying: "If I get out now I can dress in comfortable time for dinner," and a little later: "If I get out now and hurry I shall just be able to do it," and a little later: "Good Lord! There's the gong." How is it that a person who likes comfortable time for dressing before dinner cannot find power for the necessary preliminary of leaving the bath? Some people are constantly struck helpless like that all through their lives.

They read on:

Peggy's habit tapping front teeth pencil or finger nail gets on Geoffrey's nerves.

Personal charm theory. Resentment at facile dominion makes charmed beastly about and to the charmer. Charmer cannot understand. Not jealousy; beauty, wealth, wit, fame, intellect and chic are not thus resented.

Theory suffering more equal all round than at first sight as imaginary equally hard to bear.

Education theory. Only use education is, learning unrelated to own concerns and pleasure and career gives impersonal outlook, better balanced mind, and so the more useless the better.

Perdita had a terrific impression of great vitality and she stared with admiration at a pair of beautiful violet eyes and thin, long, dark eyebrows that nearly met in the middle over them. They shook hands; Perdita tried to smile with peculiar sweetness and received, as she put it, a nasty look in return. When next he met her Nigel said, sounding rather pleased than otherwise:

"You hated her, didn't you? She says you gave her a viciously nasty look!" Had she said that to be catty or did she really think it? Perhaps she had imagined it in all good faith. Then why should not Perdita herself have imagined the nasty look from her rival, who had smiled perhaps very winsomely indeed?

Later that night Claudia innocently remarked to Hugo that she and Guy had loved the bit about the nasty look.

"What? You showed him my private note-book?"

"You leave it lying about. You show it to Eileen."

For once, they had quite an unpleasant scene. Separately they gave Eileen their different slightly distorted versions after.

But all was peace next day. Later that week Hugo himself asked Guy to dine and amuse Claudia as he had a working spell on him and was poor company. Claudia and Guy went to see Nervo and Knox at the Victoria Palace and spent a divinely happy evening. They laughed and laughed, helplessly, almost painfully.

"That girl guide make up!" choked Claudia. "Knox's stringy black legs and Nervo's obscene little pigtail!"

When it was over they left still babbling to each other incoherently in terms of the play. "Cut yourself a piece of throat," "Now little boys—*and* girls—" "Simeon speaking! Don't send the barge—we'll swim 'ome." That dance at the end of the second act! That scene at the circus! They agreed how heavenly it was to be low-brow, how useless it would have been to have gone to this perfect slapstick performance with Hugo.

When they got home he was still up working and hailed Guy in for a drink.

"Oh that's what you went to see? I wish I'd gone too. I'd crawl a mile on my stomach any day to see Nervo and Knox."

Guy and Claudia exchanged unrepentant glances. He'd have been precious, patronisingly intellectual. He wouldn't have enjoyed it in the right way.

All good things come to an end, and perhaps a heroic renunciation is not the best start for a platonic friendship. The strain began to tell on

Guy and Claudia. Heavy silences fell between them, and heavier words passed. History repeated itself, and with grief and sorrow and long protest they fetched their circle round to another eternal farewell.

They talked a long time. They talked about Hugo and Carol and love and life and beauty and sacrifice and the importance of being good. Late in the day perhaps, they behaved very well. She was too shattered to realise it all at once and slept the sleep of exhaustion, but he walked about all night in his despair and the grey morning found him in the empty City with the sweat streaming down his face.

8

← →

Millions and millions of men and women in the world—all alone, all solitary and confined. ... Friends incomprehensible to each other and opaque after a lifetime of companionship ... lovers remote in one another's arms. ... The hopelessness of every passion, since every passion aims at attaining to what in the nature of things is unattainable: the fusion and interpenetration of two lives, two separate histories, two solitary and for ever sundered individualities.

ALDOUS HUXLEY.

For lo, the winter is past, the rain is over and gone; the flowers appear on the earth; the time of the singing of birds is come.

Song of Solomon.

"But what's become of your *petit monsieur*?"

"Oh we've quarrelled. I've got tired of him."

Thus Hugo and Claudia, and thus again, in different words, Claudia and Eileen. Eileen improved the occasion, giving her opinion fully and frankly. Claudia felt that she had enough to bear without Eileen's opinion.

"Gosh—she's disagreeable," she thought, "I wonder how Tommy stands it! But the answer is, she ain't disagreeable to Tommy."

Hugo said he missed Guy, and was sorry, as her next *petit monsieur* probably wouldn't be so nice.

Things went very badly for a while after this in the Lester household. Claudia could not always wholly hide her desolation, and any glimpse of weakness or of sorrow in her exasperated Hugo. He did not worry much about her conduct, he suspected no evil between her and Guy, but that was not in any case the point. He had thought that he had had her and he had never had her at all. Whoever she loved or didn't love, whatever she did or didn't do, she had broken his bubble and trodden on his dreams, and that she should be unhappy too only aggravated the offence. It might have aroused tenderness in him had he felt stronger and older than she, but there had grown up between them an unacknowledged understanding that almost all responsibilities were hers.

Unconsciously, regretfully, she accepted this. She must somehow comfort Hugo. Only she had never felt so helpless with him, almost afraid of him. Sometimes he was so withdrawn that even she seemed to become just copy, an individuality not an individual, something whose reactions he coolly studied. Most of all he resented it when she relapsed into the pretty, affected, affectionate airs and graces of earlier days. He loved them still, they moved him still, and they reminded him that he despised her.

Claudia hardly went anywhere, refusing all invitations for fear of meeting Guy. The quiet life she led further irritated Hugo, who took it as an accusation, a parade of martyrdom. She could not explain that she dared not risk enjoying the good offices of the Carstairs' set again, that her love surely went everywhere in the hope of seeing her face. And all the while this denying of a mutual love seemed such a meaningless strain, so futile a frustration. Guy possessed all her mind and all her heart; resilient though her spirits were she could not be the best of company.

Yet how much it takes to upset the even tenor of everyday life! Hugo and Claudia had so much in common they could hardly cease to be friends. It was impossible that they should be miserable all the time. They might practise bitter phrases in their minds as they lay in their baths, but when they met at breakfast or at dinner after, some joke of the old brigade would at once crop up, the items of their private daily news bulletin would require friendly, intimate discussion. Married life is so close a tie that it is not really possible to lead a two-strangers-under one-roof existence. Even Guy and his Carol with their exceptional facilities for not seeing each other hardly achieved that. Habit is so strong. It was a matter of course to Claudia to tell Hugo every little happening that seemed pleasant or amusing or touching or queer. It was a matter of course to Hugo to claim Claudia's attention to everything he wrote, and to every theory that entered his head. He might affect to himself that her fondness and liking were aggravation and insult; life without them would have been unthinkable. He was very cynical now when she petted him with his headaches and colds, but had she treated them with bracing indifference the Bank of England would have failed and the Rock of Gibraltar have sunk into the sea. Nevertheless she had injured him irreparably, and he knew quite well that she was not capable of apprehending in what wise or how much.

Hugo might have greater capacity for suffering, as being the more spiritually quickened and refined; but Claudia's trouble was far more constant and gnawing. And it was tantalising too; by this wanton act of renunciation which found no sanction in her heart or his she had deliberately bound a load of misery upon herself and upon her love. However much fun or enjoyment or work or interest she found, the longing for him was never far off from her. It lurked ready to pounce like a beast in ambush about all her ways. Morning and night her first and last thoughts were of him. Morning and night her first and last sight was his first present, a glass horse glittering and graceful on the mantelpiece, with its slim, fragile legs, its fine neck and its arrogantly posed head. She was fond of cheap music, tuneful lilting, but now the gaiety of an air would string her up temperamentally, the caress of a voice rasp suddenly on her nerves.

> What am I to do?
> I adore you!

Even the stellar lovemaking in picture palaces troubled her, so that she felt quite grateful on one occasion to a snub-nosed, pimple-faced, red-wristed, bottle-shouldered youth sitting in front of her who broke the spell by remarking, as Owen Nares passionately kissed a lady: "Coo, 'e's as bad as oi am!"

None the less, Claudia and Guy kept the sad vows they had made to each other at their second eternal farewell. They had sworn not to write or telephone and they beat the temptation down. From time to time each of them, firm in personal integrity, would will the other to fail and send a message at last. Evidently neither of them had wills sufficiently strong. And so the weeks wore away, tolerable after all since they were, in fact, tolerated.

It was between two and three months after the second eternal farewell that Hugo received by the last post a letter which caused him to exclaim with pleasure and surprise.

"Has an enemy died or have you come into money?" asked Claudia sympathetically.

"Oh well, I can't go of course. But you remember Marcel Saint-Luc?"

"I've heard you speak of him. Oh yes, and he wrote *Bonne Marchée* and *Je m'en fiche*."

"No, Esmé Desgranges wrote *Je m'en fiche*. They were all a little sort of club in Paris and they really made me one of them the year I spent there. I was one of the richer men of the party then, but now old Marcel's inherited a place and a fortune. Gosh, I haven't thought of them for years."

"I'm glad he has," cried Claudia with easily-aroused enthusiasm, "because they did give you a good time, didn't they? And it all sounds so disreputable and naughty."

"Only intellectual fun, though," twinkled Hugo.

"Je m'en fiche," she told him.

"Well, now Marcel is trying to gather us all together for a fortnight at his place. I can't go, but it's jolly to be remembered."

"But why can't you go?"

"He's forgotten I'm a married man."

"Can't you forget it too? Most people can! Gracious, I can survive two weeks by myself."

"You can't even go to Chesnor with the housemaid having whooping cough."

"Darling, you're obviously dying to go. There isn't a reason in the world why not."

"There's dozens of reasons. It's such short notice. This letter's been chasing me all over England. I'm frightfully busy. I've got tons of work and tons of engagements. Rosemary's dinner party—you know that would have been fun—and the Editor of the *Mermaid* and heaps of things."

She fetched his engagement book. She was an angel of sympathy and a tower of strength. She did all his telephone calls for him and arranged everything and booked his passage. The wish not to miss a party was one she could so thoroughly understand. Hugo was obviously thrilled about this holiday. It really didn't matter that she would lose Rosemary's pleasantly leonine dinner and spend a dreary, lonely two weeks! She smiled to think that but for her energy and sense in overcoming his difficulties Hugo would have lost his treat for no adequate reason. She felt quite a little glow of wifeliness as she finally packed him off.

Standing on Victoria Station, childishly waving a handkerchief after Hugo's train, suddenly a chill came upon Claudia. She hurried home to the Kensington house where they had planned to be so happy. She hurried home with set mouth and anxious, haunted eyes to face in quiet the sense of foreboding and disaster that lay like a heavy fog over her mind. Was it then only this, all her eager, sympathetic activity on Hugo's behalf, that she wanted to be alone and in the same town as Guy? She sat down, staring at the glass horse, fine and glittering on the mantelpiece, trying to see clearly through her doubts. What good after all would it do her that Hugo was gone? What ulterior motive could there have been in her good nature? Guy would not even know of his absence. All communications were cut off. That she would not write to him or telephone to him or send him a message or seek him out was as sure as the rising of the sun and the moon. Nevertheless not for any wealth or fame would she have left London.

For Claudia knew that somehow, somewhere, she would meet Guy. She did not speculate in her mind or wonder or hope, her foreknowledge was certain and still. She felt neither hurry nor pleasure nor suspense, just the indifferent, inevitable working of an appointed thing.

In a few minutes she got up to carry on the day's work. She had some telephone calls and some letters to do, some shops to call at, some lunches to fix with Eileen and a dinner with her and Tommy too. There was no further use in pondering over the matter. She did not even tell herself that she was not psychic, that none of her presentiments ever came true, that she was suffering from imagination, nerves, or incubating influenza. Whatever she did, wherever she went, nothing could stop her from meeting Guy.

It was not one of her many transient moods. She felt no whit altered in mind the next day. When she ran into Derek Denzel on his way to lunch at the Kit-Cat and he said: "What are you doing to-night? I wish you could come out with me as Delia's out without me and I haven't seen you for an age," she accepted, hardly even troubling to guess whether or not he was to be the instrument of her fate. They dined, saw a play and went on to the Embassy. As a matter of course, without surprise or wonder, she saw Guy sitting with a party of four.

Presently Derek stopped at their table after dancing, greeted them all and explained:

"We're consoling each other as our other halves have deserted us."

"An elopement?" someone asked.

"I don't think so. Lester's gone for a fortnight. If Delia has I shan't take her back!"

Guy and Claudia exhibited no signs of emotion. There was nothing that anyone else could notice. She smiled all round. Before she went on they exchanged a word or two in general conversation. But between them there was that strange electric current that neither of the two it binds can conceal from the other, that no one can govern or control.

A little later Guy danced with one of the two ladies of his party and then brought her up to Derek and Claudia for a moment, so that she fell into conversation with Derek and he edged Claudia a pace or two away.

"I must see you, Claudia. I've got to see you."

She said: "Yes."

"When you get home, Claudia, wait up for me a little and I'll come on as quickly as I can. I've got to see you."

Again she said: "Yes."

"Stop flirting with Guy and dance with me," demanded Derek.

Some ten minutes later she said that she was tired and asked to be taken home. She seemed composed enough, chatting pleasantly to her escort on the way, but the mood of foreboding had melted away before a surge of delight. The long separation was over and done; music clashed in her brain and the stars reeled in the sky.

She lay on the sofa in the front drawing-room waiting. She was tired. Her thoughts revolved endlessly in a sort of dream of Guy's arms about her and his face against hers in that closeness which should be but an outward symbol of the closer knitting of their hearts and minds. Two individuals whose emotions flowed as one, two personalities directed into one channel, two inseparable notes of one perfect chord; herself and Guy who should for ever understand. Her eyes were closed and she was half asleep under her dream's spell, but through it all she heard always the swish of cars, calculating their distance and direction, whether they would turn down her street, whether they were slowing up to stop. At length she heard one stop at her door and she rose and ran down. It had taken him just half an hour to break up the party, see a lady home, and come.

In the hall they stood facing each other for a moment in silence and the air seemed thick with those sweet words so soon to be told. His face was a mask that she had seen before on other men. For in some moments all men look alike. All that spoke of himself, of his own individuality, was blotted out, and there was only the expression of a universal emotion not of itself either good or evil, happy or unhappy, beautiful or debased. There seemed both strength and weakness in asking so much. The mask is always a little disturbing, and Claudia was infinitely stirred because she belonged already to the man who wore it. She turned her head a little, restlessly, to and fro on her lovely neck, with a soft, delaying, defeated smile.

9

What shall we steer by,
having no chart
but the deliberate
fraud of the heart?

HUMBERT WOLFE.

It was amazing how unexpectedly easy it was to meet Hugo again. After all, she felt so strong and happy.

After a long and merry discussion of his adventures, his primness and neatness among those wild Marcels and Esmés and Armands and Achilles, his passionately improving harangues, the feast of theory and the flow of intellect and all the ribald laughter, he asked:

"And how have you improved my absence?"

To which she answered:

"I've resurrected my *petit monsieur*!"

Thereafter things went much better in the Lesters'house in Kensington. Hugo was rather pleased to see the average man again, indeed he had quite a respect and liking for him and they could sometimes be very amusing together. Claudia positively flowered beneath the enchantment of her happiness. She was excellent company. Her occasional fits of misery were easily kept to herself, and Hugo was no more provoked by sorrow and yearning on her part. She went out often so that he could feel no more accusation and martyrdom, but not so often that he was in any way neglected. She was an attentive, companionable wife, and poor Hugo got some unsatisfactory satisfaction from despising her inferior sensibility.

Guy and Claudia were gay and popular, faithful and devoted and fairly discreet: and they became one of the accepted, almost respectable, unacknowledged liaisons of London. For fervent lovers they were wise in their generation; they tormented each other little with doubts and jealousies, they did not indulge in rows, and when they found themselves talking too much at cross purposes, either she would drop the subject, or he would resort to arguments less controvertible than words. She had yielded to him easily, but then he had not regarded her as game. She roused in him a love and protection that the constant pleasure of her society did not diminish.

Loving each other so, sometimes indeed they thought of divorce and marriage. But they never thought of it at the same time. When she wanted to run away with him, he could not possibly drag his white flower through all that. If only she were unmarried and he could get a quiet divorce on his own! But Carol was an argument too. They had been married a long time. There were old associations and memories which made Claudia feel a little stab of jealousy. He still felt some responsibility towards his wife, and little as they now meant to each other his home was yet some background to her, something stable in her life. Then, she would take even more if it weren't for him. And sometimes she got terribly depressed. Claudia had a sudden vision, so clear that she wondered if it were telepathy, of Guy in the small hours half carrying Carol to bed, supporting her trailing steps while she clung to him almost helplessly, counting the stairs up in a childish, hopeless voice, while he counted them too, encouragingly, reassuringly, like a nurse, and finally, like a nurse, put her safely to bed. Claudia felt suddenly glad that Carol should sometimes have Guy to comfort her, as she remembered her great grey eyes and the vivid, curled clusters of her golden hair.

But when it was Guy who wanted Claudia to marry him she could not contemplate the cruelty of leaving Hugo. Darling, inadequate Hugo with his smooth, girlish face and his smooth chestnut hair. He would be lost and helpless and hurt and embittered. He who would have done anything for her. Oh no, you couldn't make homes and then break them up again. And she would stick it out even if Guy were furious at her living in her husband's house and belonging in any way to another man.

One afternoon in March, a little after her twenty-eighth birthday, they sat together in the window seat of the Heseltine flat, for both her parents were at Chesnor and Guy had got home from the office early to have late tea with her alone. He was leaning back in the window, rather gracefully, holding both her hands in his.

"I love your hands. And your arms. And your shoulders. ..."

She interrupted. "I do feel happy here with you!"

"If we could be together always! If you knew how I hated your living with Hugo."

"My sweet! It's no good talking about it. Not again," she said.

"I know, darlingest. I don't want to drag you through the courts."

"It isn't only that. You see, Hugo's such a darling."

"I know. He's an awfully good fellow. Claudia, how much *do* you think he knows?"

"I can't tell. I don't think he does know, and yet in a way I feel he knows enough."

"I can't understand him, darling. He's not a fool. Yet surely if he knew about us he wouldn't stand it. How could he?"

"Perhaps artists are different. In some ways he seems a better man than you, but less of a man in others. Darling—let's not talk about Hugo, shall we?"

"Who wants to indeed?" He leant forward and drew her to him, kissing away the cloud that such speculations drew across their indeterminate happiness.

"Guy, darling, darling, do you love me as much as two years ago when we first met? As much as one year ago when I first … when we … as much as one year ago?"

"But always more, my silly little sweet."

Outside, a barrel organ played the "Blue Danube." The March sunlight streamed in with a generosity as of summer, flooding over the army of moss-bound primroses in their flat bowls and making the red, double-headed lily glow upon his stalk. Claudia noticed none of these things, taking no account of the beauty of flowers or sunlight because Guy's forehead was pressed to her forehead and they sat hand in hand.

"Isn't it strange," she said at last, "to think how one's fate and happiness are all chance? If I had happened to accept Lalage's invitation to Farling five years ago—I could have put Hugo off and I nearly did—I should have met you again for a long weekend before I was engaged. A long week-end at Farling when I was free. Oh Guy, how could I know? We can't help ourselves, it's not our fault, it's just luck, luck, all a matter of chance. If I'd chosen a different week-end visit five years ago, you and I would have been perfectly safe and happy for evermore. Unless," and her tone became a good deal lighter, "you hadn't noticed me at Lalage's at all!"

His voice was husky with the truth of his emotion.

"Beloved, if I had met you before you married—you *know* that I would never have let you go!"

PART V

TURNING TO THE RIGHT

1

Mais ne trouvez-vous pas vous-même, Aurelle reprit le Major Parker, qui l'intelligence soit estimée chez vous au dessus de sa valeur réelle? Il est certes plus utile dans la vie de savoir boxer que de savoir écrire. Vous voudriez voir Eton respecter les forts en thème? C'est comme si vous demandiez à un entraîneur de chevaux de course de s'intéresser aux chevaux de cirque.

ANDRÉ MAUROIS.

There was no one in the room. Blinds and curtains were closed; the light of the skies, if any, was shut out. There was a fire in the room: very comforting and gay. The cushions were fluffed out, inviting. An antique clock marked time in a hushed monotone. The door opened, and as Claudia came with hurried steps into the fire's glow, two open letters in her hand, the telephone began ringing. She shut the door and turned up the lights.

She crossed to the writing-table, threw down the letters and lifted the telephone receiver.

"Hullo … yes of course it is, Lalage dear … yes, longing to meet him again and the dazzling actress … how sweet of you … oh dear, but I can't! Not the week-end after next … I can't really, I'm going away already. … What fun the party sounds. … No, I really can't possibly … darling, I tell you I can't … Oh Lalage, but I can't really! … Thousands of thanks and I wish I could. … Good-bye, see you soon, Lalage!"

She sat down at the desk and began to write:

DARLING ROSEMARY—

There, she paused. She had been about to write a regretful refusal to meet Lionel Byng at Aston Cobalt the week-end after next. Wasn't it Hugo's birthday? Wasn't he counting on her? But it did seem a thousand pities to miss Rosemary's party. In the first place it would never occur again. Lionel Byng would certainly not venture among those dangerous highbrows twice. It was such an opportunity to get to know the hero, for a famous polo player who was unmarried and reported handsome would be a very pleasant addition to her circle of acquaintance. Everyone had heard of Lionel Byng; and it was probable that she would have no serious rival down at Aston Cobalt! Even if she disliked him, or at any rate failed to get on, it would surely all be inimitably funny to watch. Rosemary trying to cope with him, he trying, hopelessly puzzled, to adapt himself to his company—oh, it wasn't to be missed! Of course it didn't matter. But then Hugo could have her any time. She would go absolutely any other week-end in the year that he chose to Gloucestershire. In this letter that had just come he did seem to regard it as fixed and to write a confirmation rather than an invitation. But it had been arranged very vaguely, without even mentioning a date. Quickly she finished her letter to Rosemary:

Your S.O.S. gratefully received! I'd love to come and help tame your lion: what a glorious mixture it will all be! Thank you ever so much for asking me; I hope I may see you before then, and anyhow I'm much looking forward to it.

With love,

CLAUDIA.

Then she turned to her second letter:

DEAREST HUGO, she began,—I *am* sorry and I'd love to come

absolutely *any* week-end after. But I got in a frightful muddle … It was a difficult letter to write, and she felt rather caddish as she finished it.

Claudia arrived at Aston Cobalt just before dressing time, was warmly greeted by the family, introduced to the guests, some of whom she knew already, and then shepherded off by Rosemary to her room. Mr. Byng had not had time to get any impression of Claudia in the general flurry, but of course she had already scrutinised him.

"What do you think of my little accident?" giggled Rosemary, standing with her back to her friend's bedroom fire.

"Darling, I'd no idea he was so good-looking!" cried Claudia. "He's the most magnificent man I've ever seen. Have I missed much of him?"

"No, he arrived in a Lagonda about a quarter of an hour before you did, and in five minutes was looking both bewildered and appalled. And I don't look a bit how I looked as Cleopatra. Oh, you are an angel to come!"

"*Delighted* to oblige," said Claudia affably.

All through dinner she covertly gazed at him. He was about thirty-two and almost six foot with a real athlete's figure. His fine shoulders gave the impression that he was a heavier man than he really was. His face was astonishingly handsome. He was very dark. He had black hair, very slightly curling, black eyebrows and moustache, a Spanish complexion, a slightly aquiline nose, and a beautifully cut mouth that in smiling showed excellent white teeth. But most striking of all were his eyes. He had no foreign blood, but his dark, dark brown eyes were such as you seldom see in an Englishman's face. Dark and deep and sad and lazy, they seemed in repose to speak of some mystery, not lightly to be revealed. This mystery, this romance in his eyes was incongruous and intriguing in a straightforward, stupid, sporting man.

For stupid he was, as Claudia found out in a very little conversation at dinner. She sat next him, but the lady on his other side had recently received a revelation about a curious, pantheistic form of religion to which she was anxious to make a convert. He was naturally unable to refute any of her arguments, and this encouraged her so that he got all too little chance to refresh himself with Claudia's chitchat on golf. He did however mark her down as the one human being there.

After dinner when the gentlemen had joined the ladies, Rosemary dealt round pencils and half sheets.

"We'll play 'Reviews.' You know, each time you've written a sentence you double back that section of paper, and each pass your sheet to the right-hand neighbour. First the name of the book, then the alternative name, then the author, then the publisher, then what Gerald Gould said of it, what Harold Nicholson said of it and what Ralph Straus said of it. Shall we have what the man in the street said as well?"

The dark, sad eyes of the great polo player met Claudia's in entreaty, and she felt she knew exactly what the man in the street said.

"Come along and play ping pong with me, somebody," urged Claudia persuasively. "Mr. Byng, will you come and play ping pong?"

They adjourned together to the oak room. She thought it the pleasantest in the house. It was sparsely furnished, but round the fire there were deep, comfortable armchairs, and for the rest there was chiefly the ping pong table, the gramophone and records, and a space of polished floor. It was panelled with light, unstained oak except for some shelves of books, and on winter evenings a big log fire generally blazed. In front of this they sat to rest after Mr. Byng had won two out of three hard-fought games.

She asked: "Have you known Rosemary long?"

So he told her all about the fancy dress dance and how jolly and ordinary Rosemary had seemed as Cleopatra and how he'd never seen her natural self till now.

"She seems a nice sort of girl," he said discontentedly.

"Oh, Rosemary's a dear."

"She's a bit clever, though, isn't she?"

"Not very," pleaded Claudia loyally.

He persisted in his complaint. "I think she is. They seem to me a very clever sort of crowd altogether."

"I think they are rather. I can't tell you what the man on my other side at dinner was like. He kept talking about modern French art, and he might have been interesting but he lisps *and* stutters. All the same he wouldn't let me get a word in edgewise. The extraordinary thing is that though I'd nothing to say I kept vainly trying to get words in edgewise and being furious that I couldn't."

"When I tell you that my female talked of nothing but God you'll know what sort of an evening I had. I *am* glad you're here, Miss Heseltine!"

When they returned to the others Rosemary was suggesting a paper game in which you chose quotations from literature to advertise various well-known trade commodities.

"Don't they ever play bridge?" whispered Lionel Byng wistfully.

"That *is* a good idea! Rosemary darling, *couldn't* we get up a bridge four?"

"Why Claudia," cried Rosemary, "you know you like paper games ever so much better than bridge."

Claudia was so amiably adaptable that in time past this had sometimes actually been the case. But she passed it off very well. She said:

"Of course I love your paper games, Rosemary darling," in a voice of patent insincerity and winked at her cavalier.

All the next day Lionel Byng clung to Claudia as to a lifebelt, and all the next day she looked at his broad shoulders and his white teeth and his dark eyes, and rejoiced. The rest of the house party thought she was being noble and that it was very funny; they even urged her not to be quite so unselfishly noble. This advice she ignored.

Lionel Byng had not a great deal to say for himself to girls. He was a thorough man's man, at the same time he was used to being spoilt on account of his looks and fame by charming wives and divorcées who did all the work for him. Claudia reflected that it would have been grossly unfair if so fine a man as Lionel Byng should also have been as easy to talk to as all the nice, intelligent squits. And the two of them got on very well together. They talked about travel and Scotland and how nice it would be if it were summer and they could run over to the sea and bathe, and on the Saturday morning they had a round of golf. As the glamour of Cleopatra and the fancy dress dance faded further away, Lionel Byng was more than ever at a loss to understand how he could have accepted an invitation from a strange girl—and such a girl! But in spite of everything it was a lucky chance. For it had brought him to Claudia.

He had never taken much notice of a girl before, that is, since he was a good deal younger. Now there was no tolerable alternative. And curiously enough he wanted no alternative. Taking notice of Claudia was a singularly pleasant occupation. She seemed so different, so innocent and flower-like and gay.

After dinner on Saturday Rosemary and a few of her guests evolved another idea for general entertainment. This was to have a mock debate. The question chosen was to be argued with as much solemnity and feeling as could be achieved.

"What's it all about?" Mr. Byng asked nervously of Claudia.

"They're going to have a debate on 'To be or not to be.' One's going to argue in favour of enduring life and another of escaping from it, and there'll be a good deal of heckling and general chitchat."

He shuddered. "Well, if they're going to act according to the result of the meeting, I hope 'not to be' will have it and they'll all commit suicide!"

Claudia laughed in hearty appreciation. Then:

"Should we sneak off to the oak room," she suggested, "and dance?"

He danced very well in the unenergetic, slide-and-hesitate style. Held closely to him, anchoring herself securely to one of the shoulders she so admired, Claudia closed her eyes and danced in a quiet ecstasy.

His comment, after they had played through several records and come to rest in front of the roaring fire, was,

"Warm work this! I'll say we've earned a drink."

However she was not at all discouraged for she knew quite well he had liked dancing with her. In a sudden burst of friendship she told him how Rosemary had misheard their introduction and taken him for the artist Dion Dring, and how she had subsequently sent her, Claudia, a piteous appeal. He laughed over this mistake, and then, suddenly remembering, he said rather acutely:

"What did you mean last night asking me if I hadn't known Rosemary for ages, when you knew all about everything?"

"Oh well, I was just making conversation. I didn't guess we'd get to be such friends I should tell you secrets."

"Not much of a secret. Tell me another."

"Are you to be trusted, Mr. Byng?"

"Yes—Miss Heseltine. Try and see—Miss Heseltine."

"All right—Lionel! I don't see why I shouldn't. I'll tell you one. You see ..."

"Well?"

"No, I can't really."

"Tell me."

"No, I don't think I can."

"But you promised."

"I will when I know you better."

"How am I to get to know you better?"

Claudia still couldn't think of anything on earth to tell him and failed still to invent an adequate secret. So she said, gazing back into his deep, now rather ardent eyes:

"What about you? Haven't you any secrets to tell me?"

"I might tell you one to-night. I shan't be able to keep it secret long, Claudia!"

They stood looking very consciously at each other for a few seconds, then he put on the gramophone again and they danced, more than ever tightly jammed together like a couple of sardines on a spree. They danced on and on, dreamily, happily. At last they came to rest in front of the fire.

"Dion Dring! An artist!" said Lionel, and they both burst into a hearty roar of laughter. It certainly did seem funny. Presently he resumed:

"Soft job, that, painting good-looking women all your life and getting paid for it."

"Oh, artists get so much of looks they think nothing of them," explained Claudia airily. "*Nothing's* a treat to an artist."

He nodded, and concluded, looking interested and rather solemn:

"I know. Just think of them painting a pretty girl in the nude and thinking nothing about it."

Indeed he felt quite strongly on the subject of art. For at Sunday lunch the subject cropped up again, and Rosemary's friends talked eagerly of Renoir and Gauguin. And, "Van Gogh," they said, "you know his flower paintings are so intense that they almost frighten one."

And "Picasso," they said, "do you know that wonderful drawing of his of an elbow three times the natural size? The pores of the skin! The hairs! Superlative!"

They spoke of a one man exhibition here and a gallery there, and as they spoke of galleries, Lionel Byng, who had listened in silence, suddenly uttered his one art criticism.

"Madonnas!" he said. "My God!"

Claudia's heart warmed at this touch of nature.

On Sunday afternoon Lionel Byng slept in the oak room until tea, and Claudia just sat and looked at him with much the same pleasure that you might feel in watching some great, beautiful animal at the Zoo. He was magnificent, like a tiger. In just the same way it was a little awe-inspiring to see him with his strength relaxed, unconscious of scrutiny, his senses all unaware. When at last he yawned and stretched and awoke, the illusion, instantly to be dispelled, was almost complete.

Later they danced together again alone. One new tune they encored and encored.

> I like you very much, but not so much as I did before,
> And I believe there was a time you used to love me more.
> I wouldn't hurt you for the world—but I'm feeling terribly sold!
> What are we going to do now love's grown cold?

Not very helpful words, but the tune was catchy and maddening. Suddenly he stopped in the middle of the floor, his arms still holding her to him, and said:

"It wouldn't ever grow cold, would it?"

She stirred restlessly and said:

"What are you talking about?"

"I'm talking about us. I've never loved anyone quite like this before. Can't we get married? I know I'm not much of a chap and all that. Not fearfully bright perhaps—"

"Oh, Lionel, you are!"

"But I generally get what I want and I want you frightfully. Do be nice to me."

"Do you—generally get what you want, Lionel?"

"Always."

"Then it's no good my arguing, is it?"

"Gosh! Do you love me too?"

"I adore you, Lionel."

"You are a good looker, Claudia."

"Lionel—would you love me as much if I weren't pretty?"

"No, of course I wouldn't. Why?"

"Oh nothing. It's jolly of you to own it."

"Damn it all, you are pretty."

"Yes, I am, aren't I? Oh, Lionel."

"Darling. We're going to be awfully happy. I'll give you every damn thing you want."

"I don't want anything. Just you."

"Well, call that nothing!"

"Oh, Lionel."

"Darling. I am happy. You're beautiful, Clau. Are you happy too?"

"Yeh. I'm all right!"

They were settled by now, very much all right, in one of the armchairs. He held her tenderly, protectively. She was so slight and wonderful and young. And leaning against him with her eyes closed she yet saw his eyes, dark and romantic, deep with a secret sadness and surely some reserve of mystery hidden from the world. She felt almost faint with happiness and excitement.

"God, this is grand!" said Lionel.

2

←→

Ah, the long road! And you so far away!
Oh, I'll remember! But ... each crawling day
Will pale a little your scarlet lips, each mile
Dull the dear pain of your remembered face.

RUPERT BROOKE.

From Miss Claudia Heseltine to Mr. Hugo Lester.

HUGO DEAREST,—I hardly know how to tell you my news. It does seem so awful that a thing like this should happen to me without you and Eileen, my two most beloved friends in the world, knowing a thing about it. You will believe that I wouldn't ever have had secrets from you, because you see I couldn't have known myself. I can't understand how anything so important could happen so quickly, so wonderfully, all out of the blue. Hugo, I'm going to marry Lionel Byng. I'm so happy and he is so sweet.

Here there followed a sentence which, on re-reading the letter, she thought better of. She had already re-written the thing once owing to blurring the first part with sudden, unaccountable tears. So this time she merely scrawled out the offending sentence by writing the word "apples" over and over again on top. This is usually an efficient method, but she blotted it immediately in her haste so that it was much lighter than the dried ink underneath.

I'm longing to see you as soon as possible. It seems too bad that neither you nor Eileen can be a bridesmaid! Lionel and I are going to give lots of parties after, and some of them are to be the sort you and Rosemary will like. He's not a bit intellectual, but he's interested in art, though he doesn't know anything about it, and he often reads, and one person's as likely as another to be right about a book. I mean it's a matter of taste in a way. Of course really he's just the sweetest, most divine, complete nitwit! But he is wonderful and I'm so thrilled. Rosemary's a sort of friend of his too, so we can all have heaps of fun together. I can't get on with this letter a bit, it's all turning out rubbish, but Hugo dear, I wanted you to be the first to know, and I'm telling you before even Eileen and the parents, so I suppose you must be my best friend of all!

With ever so much love,

CLAUDIA.

From Mr. Hugo Lester to Miss Claudia Heseltine.

CLAUDIA MY DEAR,—Your letter was certainly unexpected, but then to be unexpected is one of the canonised charms of your sex. By the way, the super-inscribed apples over the sentence you wished to delete were too quickly blotted, so I need hardly tell you that I took your letter to a good light and made the sentence out. Well! No wonder you blushed for shame and repented on re-reading so masculine a sentiment as "I do hope you and Lionel will like each other and be the greatest friends"! Here in exchange is a feminine sentiment for you. Of course it's only your point of view, your life I think of; that's all that matters; I hope you're going to be very, very happy—but by God if you are ...!

I do congratulate you with all my heart. Everyone tells me he's a Prince of Good Fellows in the best British Tradition and I fervently hope you'll be very happy always. I think this necessitates his being happy too, though it would have been jolly if you could have seen your way to leading him a dog's life! I am going round the world and am very much thrilled about it. Will you forgive me if I don't come and say good-bye to you? You know, I don't believe we *can* go on "being friends." I'm sorry and you're not to feel hurt about it. We Lesters were ever a peevish family and I don't fancy standing god-parent to any of your little sportsmen and sportswomen. God bless you, darling.

All my love,

Hugo.

P.S. It will be fun, you know, to be my own man again.

3

I would have sworn, indeed I swore it:
The hills may shift, the waters may decline,
Winter may twist the stem from the twig that bore it,
But never your love from me, your hand from mine.

EDNA ST. VINCENT MILLAY.

Ye take too much upon ye, ye sons of Levi.

MOSES.

Lionel Byng was immensely eligible, and immensely popular too through his polo prowess and being rich, handsome, good-natured and sociable. The Heseltine parents found him very genuinely likeable. They were much surprised and puzzled by the engagement, but they were pleased as the two seemed so happy. All her friends poured congratulations upon Claudia on this very triumphant occasion. All except Eileen. She was bitterly indignant and upset. Lionel and Tommy liked each other mildly, could have played an occasional round of golf. Lionel liked Eileen, putting down all her rudeness imperviously as chaff. But she could not control her irritation at and scorn of him. She could not hold her tongue on the subject to Claudia. Claudia bore criticism of his intellect very well, merely laughing and protesting that she didn't care, that he was altogether lovable and a perfect dear. But she could not stand her friend's anxiety to snub him, and most of all she resented the violent, shocked accusation that what she felt for Lionel was not fit to be called love, that she was selling her soul for so many pounds of meat. And on this point they had their first and final serious quarrel. Each unjustifiable thing that was said hurt each equally. And though the longing to comfort her soon drove Claudia round to Eileen with words of warmth and love and peace, and a reconciliation was effected, though they forgave each other the actual quarrel, they could not quite forgive the causes of it. Thereafter their ways lay more and more apart.

The engagement was an unhappy time for Claudia, on account of the estrangement from her two best friends. With Lionel she was generally thrilled and happy, but she was tired and therefore nervy throughout this period, with the rush and bustle of arrangements and work and the approaching upheaval of all the life she knew. The evening before her wedding day her mother seemed to be preparing to tell her facts unknown to her of sinister import. But she felt she could stand no more, and anyway it was too late now. So she staved off the information by pretending she already knew.

It was a vast, very fashionable London wedding. Claudia glowed with excitement and pride, people stared and chattered and some prayed. While the register was being signed, boys' voices sang in exquisite indifference: "Love one another with a pure heart fervently, see that ye love one another." Eileen bowed her golden head upon her hands too dully, coldly unhappy to pray or cry. She had meant to be even more unhappy than she was, but the thought of Tommy kept flitting officiously, comfortingly across her mind.

Claudia cried quite stupendously, torrentially upon her honeymoon. But she cried for the most part on Lionel's shoulder, so neither of them found it too bad.

4

I launched into an apostrophe. "Oh Divine House Opposite!"
I cried, "Charming House Opposite! What is a man's own
dull, uneventful home compared with that Glorious House
Opposite! If I might dwell for ever in the House Opposite!"
...
I went downstairs, and in absence of mind, bade my cabman
drive me to the House Opposite. But I have never got there.

The Dolly Dialogues, ANTHONY HOPE.

Lionel and Claudia returned from their honeymoon via Paris to
Mayfair, where they installed themselves in a commodious house, and
life was very good. It did not occur to Claudia as strange that so splendid
a specimen of manhood as her husband should do nothing whatever for
his country beyond playing polo. She had a slight prejudice in favour of
regular work for men, but still if you had so much money it was perhaps
more logical to spend it than to make more.

How proud she was of him! Of his looks, of his fame, of his popularity.
Nothing was pleasanter than to bask in the sun at Ranelagh watching
him play. Well, of course, many things were pleasanter. It was pleasanter
still to sit on his knee of an evening and lisp to him, calling him Toto
and being called Puss-pussy. She thought sometimes with shame
of how Eileen would despise this, not knowing that alas! there were
moments when even Tommy was Mr. Borstal Boy, even Eileen Mrs.

Umperty-Pooh. It was pleasant too to be envied and to burst continually into all the papers as the beautiful Mrs. Byng. Lionel was such a solid, satisfactory achievement, and when she was not in the mood for solid satisfaction she could gaze into the depths of his dark, unfathomable, foreign eyes, and dream that there was really a mystery there for her to unravel.

They were extremely hospitable, as well they might be. It was jolly to find that the light-hearted Alan Vane was a great friend of Lionel's, and he knew many others of the Carstairs set, including the Verneys. Claudia met Guy's lovely actress wife at last, saw her slouching about all beautiful and rounded, flashing her jewels, heard her wake up after supper and many drinks and become *risqué* and shrill. Lionel rather liked Carol but would not join Claudia in being sorry for her. He said he supposed that she suited herself. Alas, how many of us with no other aim in view, with no conflicting currents, ever achieve that! But they saw more of Guy than Carol. Claudia wondered why he should be considered attractive. He was nothing very special, she thought. Not magnificent like Lionel, not intellectual like Hugo, not sparkling like Alan. But there was sometimes between them an odd, vague flicker of pleasure and warmth as though, if they had spent more time and more trouble, they might have been real friends.

Claudia enjoyed herself thoroughly in Lionel's circle. But though they were for the most part a good deal cleverer than he, she did sometimes thirst for the refreshment of intellectual society. They sometimes saw something of Rosemary Crane, but he was rather once-bitten-twice-shy about her in spite of the good turn she had done him, and several times they struck it unlucky, finding her pick-ups undeniably ticks. Both enjoyed their occasional visits to Chesnor, though even there Lionel sometimes found himself out of his depth. On the other hand his rare incursions into deep arguments were rather lovable. There was a great discussion of religion and the Church one week-end into which he suddenly broke with the surprising statement that *all* parsons were mischievous, meddling, snobbish, narrow-minded, hidebound hypocrites.

"But darling," protested Claudia, "they're the most hard-working, underpaid, unselfish people. How many parsons have you known?"

"None, thank God!" said Lionel.

Much as Claudia wished that he had a greater range of ideas, a wider variety of interests and more knowledge of feminine psychology, his conversation as well as his beautifully proportioned bulk had great charm for her. And he was so generous, so sweet, so anxious to be kind. Turning to him for sympathy she would get, not perhaps what she wanted, but always something. Towards the end of the first year of marriage she read of the sudden death of an old flowerwoman she had dealt with slightly, and who the newspapers now told her had once been a famous singer and dancer named Lou Delane. It was hurting to think of the old hag with her bleared eyes, her roughened voice and the somewhat coarse raillery that flowed from her mouth in the odour of alcohol, and then to see these ancient, resurrected photographs of a lithe, radiant creature with a tantalising smile and a halo of curls. She was dead in her rags and dirt, knocked down drunk in the street, she who had swayed packed houses night after night in the days of her triumph, who had delighted so many men, loving them neither wisely nor well to the tune of their emeralds and pearls. Claudia was all overcome and upset because she had actually known her, spoken to her lately, and she poured it out, all that was glamorous, all that was sordid, in an incoherent wail to Lionel.

"Solemn thing, death," said Lionel.

"I saw her only the other day," she told him shakily.

He nodded thoughtfully. "Life hangs by a thread!" announced Lionel. She kissed the top of his head and cheered up completely, sitting on his knee with her arms round his neck to tell him that she loved him better than anyone in the world.

It was very pleasant, that first year of marriage. Claudia blossomed out a good deal and wore beautiful clothes. She entertained all his old flames constantly, and automatically liked them all. There was polo in the summer and hunting in the winter, a bit of racing, a bit of yachting, a bit of shooting, trips abroad to fashionable pleasure resorts, and parties, heavens! how many parties! She saw herself in a sort of panic twenty years later still bound to the same wheel, still rather enjoying it, with Lionel grown a little bored and heavy but unable to contemplate any other sort of life. It was all so stereotyped, so eternally the same, and yet she genuinely did love dancing and clothes and smart society. Sometimes she felt lonely with Lionel and horribly missed Eileen. He hadn't got Hugo's intellect or high-mindedness, nor Guy Verney's soothing intelligence, nor Alan Vane's entertaining flow of charming high spirits tempered with pleasant, shallow sentimentality. How could you really exchange ideas with Lionel? Was the mystery of his wonderful, deep, dark eyes purely a physical trait? Left to his own resources he didn't know how to amuse himself, and if he didn't get enough exercise he was depressed and bored. When all went well he was a magnificent specimen and rather a dear.

Lionel was very sweet to Claudia when she was expecting her child. He took to reading aloud to her, badly but not unintelligibly, simple, rousing classics of schoolroom days, and the Book Society's novels. They seemed to get closer together, and when the child was born, eighteen months after their marriage, she was surprised and delighted to find that she did, contrary to all her expectations, dearly and immediately love her tiny son. They named him Alan and made Alan Vane godfather because he would be so easy to get things out of. They put the baby down for Eton, or, as they jocularly stated, Narkover.

"I want him to do a job of work, darling," said Claudia, cuddling the small, infinitely soft bundle, "and not be a parasite like us."

"Oh, he'll have to work when he grows up," said Lionel. "The

Government will have snaffled all our money by then. I think I should bring him up to be a gigolo and then he'll be certain to be able to support us in comfort."

Darling little Alan! It was all true, the incredible stuff you heard talked about babies and motherhood. He was fascinating and wholly individual. No other baby in the world would do. After nursing him three months it was delightful to get back to the gay round she had been despising, and she was no longer wholly dependent on the gay round for interest and occupation. She no longer worried much about having no one to go to concerts and galleries with her, needing support, for she was not intellectual enough to go alone. With Lionel and young Alan and health and wealth it is not surprising that she was very well contented with life. And yet there seemed a waste space in it; something that had never woken or had fallen asleep.

5

⬅ ➡

The loneliest associations are those that pretend to intimacy.

THORNTON WILDER.

Claudia never wholly lost an awed, fascinated interest in the size of Lionel's breakfasts.

"And yet during the rest of the day you're rather a small eater. You must hoard it up like a camel or something."

"How do you mean, a camel?"

"Oh you know, camels. They've got a rather nifty arrangement of four stomachs."

Lionel shook his head. "I couldn't afford that after the last budget."

He got up and returned presently from the sideboard with a poached egg.

"Have this, Clau?"

"No thanks, darling."

"Go on, do. Do you good."

"I can't cope with much breakfast after last night. Even my roll isn't going down too well."

"Making things flap and turn over, what? Never mind, as long as it stays down. I may as well keep this egg now I've got it. I'm not feeling too good myself."

"I've got an awful head, Lionel."

"Mine's worse."

"Mine keeps opening and shutting."

"Mine's going to blow up."

"We *must* get to bed early. What are we doing to-night, darling?"

"Dining with the Denzels, aren't we, Clau?"

She leant forward, full of the vulgar curiosity which the affairs of others excite in the sympathetic mind.

"Do you think the Denzels are happy?"

There was a long, concentrated pause.

"What?" said Lionel.

"The Denzels, darling. Do you think they're happy?"

"Never asked them."

"But do you think they are?"

"How do you mean, happy?"

"You know, happy. Like you and me."

"Oh ah, yes, I see. I should think they're all right."

"But all that bickering and fighting and jealousy and rows."

"Oh, I see what you mean. I don't suppose they are."

"It would make us miserable, darling. And yet I don't know about them. It keeps them very interested in each other and I don't think they mind."

"People are different," said Lionel, making an intelligent effort. And after a further second's thought: "Some people enjoy a scrap." And after a trifle more of consideration: "I've known chaps who've never been so happy as out in France in the war."

"Perhaps that was because of knowing exactly what was expected of them?" she suggested.

"I've no idea."

"You don't suffer from them, do you?"

"Chaps who enjoyed the war? No, why should I?"

"No, from ideas, sweet stupid."

Lionel looked a little aggrieved and replied: "I like a good talk."

She laughed and observed: "Oh Lord, my head!" And they relapsed into the papers.

"Politics," said Claudia a little timidly, for they were not her strong point, "seem in a grand muddle, don't they?"

"It's these damned Socialists," he assured her, "and anyway no one ever gets a big enough majority now to do anything. Government by party's cracking up. I'd abolish it, Pussy."

"And what would you do then?"

Lionel appeared to be considering and then said, "What?"

She went on, "I mean in the present state of things could one man do much under his own steam? You'd think we might produce *one* man; but could one individual do much for the country now?"

"Well, if he's the right man. This chap Robinson for instance, seems pretty confident he'll beat the American record."

They read on.

"By Jove!" cried Lionel, "Billy Irvine has won the amateur rackets championship again after all. Good old Billy. Awful good chap, Billy."

"Darling, surely he's a fearful brute. He's not a good chap is he, really?"

"He plays lovely rackets."

"But you don't like him, do you? I thought he was a rather nasty rotter."

"Well it's mood you know. Sometimes he does play some very funny rackets. Just doesn't try." He read on and resumed: "I say, this Chadleigh murderer must have been a bit off it. Apparently after he'd done her in he first tore all her clothes off—"

"Oh, I'm not reading that one. It's too beastly. Shut up!"

"—And then started peeling her face—"

"*Shut up*, Toto! I feel sick already to-day."

"No, but do listen, and then—"

"Lionel, if you go on I'll smash your front teeth. I *won't* be purified by pity and terror."

"How do you mean, purified?"

"Oh darling, I do love you. What should I do without you?"

"Well that's all right, darling. I'm stopping on!"

"Lionel—seeing tragedies and things, do you think it's really emotional luxury and sensationalism?"

"What—oh, I see what you mean. Ought you to enjoy your good cry, or ought you to be a strong silent girl?"

"I don't mean anything of the sort. I mean, is there anything in being purified by pity and terror?"

"Well," said Lionel, looking disgusted, "I should hate you to be any purer." And he began to whistle "The old grey mare is not what she used to be."

Claudia blew him a kiss.

6

I began to think that I should never be able to hate or ridicule any of mankind, if, in imagination, I first shared their childhood with them. "From his power to see children in men sprang that unique quality in Christ's judgment which was not what we call justice nor what we call mercy," I thought. ... Other men ... are not to blame: they must conduct the world as it is; they are its administrators, not the givers of truth to it. When a judge sends a murderer to be hanged, he does what he must. ... If each criminal stood his trial in his own nursery there could be neither prison nor gallows.

...

I am beginning to see what it is that gives moral, as well as aesthetic, beauty to a great painting or a great poem, however debased its subject may be. A great artist perceives beneath all concealments that innocency of life which is the only background capable of exhibiting the truth of pain, of joy, of each human experience. In the criminal, he perceives one who formerly was guiltless; in the harlot, maidenhood; in age, youth. Portraying the flesh he discovers the origin and the journey of the soul.

Portrait in a Mirror, CHARLES MORGAN.

Claudia wandered round Hyde Park exercising Lionel's dogs one morning when she had been married nearly three years. She loved her child, was fond of her husband, had a good time, money, friends, and no enemies. She had also much *joie de vivre*, so it was merely because the sun had gone in and the February morning had turned bitterly cold that a mood of black sadness had come upon her.

She began impersonally with the Cazlitt divorce. In regard to this sordid affair there were just two schools of thought. She herself and her friends belonged to the one which forgave all concerned because they didn't care, because it didn't matter, because scandals were beneficial to conversation. Eileen, and even Mr. and Mrs. Heseltine, belonged to the other which held that the principals in the affair were trash and poison whom decent people should cut. The first attitude was so patently unidealistic and wrong that Claudia had assumed that the rival camp, to which she could never belong, were entirely right. But they were wrong too.

How could you think as she did that the Cazlitts' behaviour had no importance, that the example they had given, the things they had done to each other, most of all the things they had done to their own minds, didn't matter, and could be overlooked? And yet you couldn't sit with Eileen and just condemn. For how they suffered. Lady Gilda Cazlitt, who had married in ignorance at seventeen a man of the world who had broken her ignorance with a hammer. She had fought hard before the world defeated her: even now she had not lost her courage with her illusions, and possessed many genuine principles which she used as whitewash. Sir Reggie Cazlitt himself, that coarse prince of good fellows and hard livers, with all his loud laughter, how tragic his face looked now if you saw it in repose. He had fallen below his own standards and he knew it, and what a fate to have to marry Mrs. Joyce! And even Sybil Joyce, man-eater, drug-fiend, shrew, how painful had been her journey since the days when she ran away from her governess to go cowslipping and birds'-nesting, not minding if she scratched her face or tore her clothes. Now she loved Reggie desperately, body and soul, and was a slave to her drug, and cried and shivered every night at the haunting terror of death.

Of course it was their own fault. They could have helped it. It came of God's great gift of free will, His high compliment, His outsize gamble. They started imperceptibly, almost harmlessly down the slope, oh, so far back! It hurt you so to go on kicking against the pricks as the young do, but when you gave it up, look what in the end muddle and drift could do to you. People needn't be stupid, people could look. Surely too the fortunate of the earth, the blest and the favoured with this world's advantages, had the greater responsibility. Surely more self-control could fairly be demanded of the educated rich. And now, it was wrong to condone and it was wrong to condemn. But surely it took Christ Himself fervently both to love the sinner and hate the sin.

Another problem. If a better woman than Gilda, a pure and charming woman, had been married to Reggie, what should she have done? A quotation came to mind, but vaguely and incoherently, so that we must set it out for Claudia.

> *Charmian*: In each thing give him way, cross him in
>   nothing.
> *Cleopatra*: Thou teachest like a fool: the way to lose him.
> *Charmian*: Tempt him not so too far: I wish, forbear;
>   In time we hate that which we often fear.

Yes! On one or other of those rocks, how many women had foundered! If you were exacting and difficult and made scenes, he went to someone who seemed pleased to see him and was pleasant when he came. If you never asked questions or kept him up to the mark but felt it was hard if a man couldn't have his fun, as she would do, you made it too easy for human frailty to go further than it meant down the primrose path. He might even despise you.

Well, thank God these questions didn't arise between her and Lionel. How lucky she was to have him and small Alan, now a year and a half old and quite adorable. They ought to have another some time. And yet, alas, since no baby could be sweeter or better loved than Alan and he for all the interest she took in him could not fill her life, another baby would not fill it either, only crowd the same compartment of it, leaving one untenanted still. Children couldn't fill your life. And that was well for you and them, since they wanted you so much when you were young and strong and not at all when it was your turn to cling to them.

And on this saddest reflection the sun came out. All the, not sad but blank, slightly anxious faces around, lit up with quick happiness. It was a day of real spring, suddenly warm and golden, a morning of buds reaching out to the light, of tiny birds replenishing the earth with their romances. Claudia, who seldom had black moods, stood still a moment in conscious thanksgiving at the shattering of this one. Then she laughed and began to run towards the waterfall at the west end of the Serpentine, heading for the Row. And she paused before the waterfall, and there was a heron and seven rabbits. And when she went on she literally walked into Hugo whom she had not seen for almost three years.

"Oh Hugo," she cried, "look, there are seven rabbits!"

Hugo, seeing that joyous face, forgot all his bitterness, and counted and said:

"Silly! There are eight."

7

> It seemed somehow unfair—as though there were no pleasing
> conscience whatever one did. Conscience might have retorted
> that in some situations there is no "right thing"; there is a bold
> but fatal thing, and there is a prudent but shabby thing; the
> right thing has vanished earlier in the proceedings.
>
> ANTHONY HOPE.

It was quite, quite wonderful to find Hugo again. At last an outlet
for profitless abstract speculations, at last a companion for concerts, a
companion for walks. Lionel was very sweet and understanding about
him. He really liked Hugo, and it seemed so amazingly jolly that
Claudia's intellectual leanings should have picked on such a decent,
almost normal fellow, whose intelligence really hardly spoilt him at all.
Then she didn't neglect her husband, didn't go out without him much.
The Byngs had a strongly domestic streak and knew that much separate
gadding is the beginning of the end.

Oh, but it was nice, it was nice to walk and talk and argue with Hugo!
His pride defeated, he had come back at last to scold and lecture her as
of old. Nothing was too trivial to start him off.

And he would only laugh too over Claudia's surprise and delight at
having a child being really so thrilling. She told him:

"When he was quite small, you know, you'd think seeing a baby once
was enough for two months! But it isn't. It's fascinating. At least half of

what they tell you beforehand is true. I never thought I'd love him better than the dogs!"

Hugo wasn't especially fond of children and wouldn't be at all touched at Lionel's love for them.

"Of course your own's different," he informed Claudia, "but why you should be proud of Lionel's loving children as such I can't think. They're pretty well as varied as grown ups. And look at the sort of people children like. Never the sensitive person, the dreamer, the poet. The sort of man all children adore is Reggie Cazlitt."

"Poor Reggie! He is so generous," murmured Claudia, thereby rashly furnishing a text for a capital short sermon.

Hugo had such vitality. Twice Lionel's vitality. So gorgeously quick in the uptake. He was interested in everything. Every funny little thing she told him. And he could be serious and sympathetic about the stupidest worries. Maybe a rather smart and elderly dinner party she was giving. Maybe her sudden vision of Botticelli's "Birth of Venus," of something touching and disturbing in her face. Love-and-Beauty coming in innocence, ignorance and wonder ashore, not knowing all that man should do unto her. Yet troubled by some dim foreknowledge; her eyes asking a question, as well they might.

Claudia was never possessive (fortunate Lionel and young Alan) and would not have encroached on Hugo's work even if he would have permitted it. He was working well and hard, but discussions and holidays with his old friend seemed to him to help him. Very often Lionel was there and his presence was no embarrassment. He and Hugo were rather jolly together chaffing each other. Claudia took great care that Lionel shouldn't feel left out of much of her life. Under the new circumstances it was easier than ever to be nice to him, because she no longer wanted to turn to him with demands he could not fulfil. Altogether it seemed hard that Eileen should, on one of their now rather rare meetings, take her to task about it. It was excessively tiresome, yet she was touched. It seemed so like old days.

"But darling, you know friendship's my one ideal. I'd never get in his way when he started a girl to marry; I'm not jealous or exacting. Eileen, don't try to take anything away from me again!"

But Eileen was very disagreeable and scornful. Thus for a moment they recaptured a past flavour, and Claudia hugged her at parting and Eileen hugged back again and both protested: "I love you always—you know that, don't you?" But it wasn't any good. They were calling to each other across a widening gulf, and anyway Mr. Byng was quite too much for Eileen.

Of course Eileen's words of foreboding had no effect at all on the Hugo-Claudia relationship. He was allowed to come unchecked. He used to drop in for tea and read his works. Lionel was allowed to listen when he wanted to and even threw out criticisms as a half-intentional joke—"Your people talk too much," or "What I like in a book is blood." Often to relax his mind Hugo would march Claudia and the dogs round the Park, talking rubbish with his usual gusto.

One evening that they had planned to go to a concert they suddenly decided to go instead to the Chelsea Palace. Here for the first time Claudia saw Mr. Ernest Lotinga.

The piece was well acted and produced. It went as slick as butter. Everyone spoke very much faster than actors in the West End, and this didn't seem at all a bad idea. Claudia felt an awful doubt at the opening jokes as to whether she was going to enjoy herself. Such a pleasantry as "Are you Mr. Tar?" "No, my name's Black." "Well, tar's black, isn't it?" left her utterly dumbfounded. But after the discovery in the German spy's luggage of a pair of stays on which Ernie Lotinga played the concertina, the show never looked back. Quite apart from such gems as the unsolicited testimonial "You're a white man, sir—except your neck," the thing was a crescendo of absurdity. And how well the actors all did their stuff.

"What different types of humour there are," said Claudia rather platitudinously in the interval, idly watching advertisements jerkily drawing themselves one after another in black upon the white screen. "And isn't it jolly the way they plug their jokes? I suppose *Private Lives* would be a complete flop here."

"I've seen Ernie funnier really even than this," boasted Hugo, "there's a show where he's chucked out of the police force and becomes a private detective. He has a perfect fool-proof case to clear his client, but unfortunately he's called to give evidence just in the very middle of his lunch. All he can do in the witness box is to spray the judge with chewed biscuit, and oh, how many crumbs that man did spray. It was a treat," Hugo assured her earnestly, "to see how he could spray that judge with biscuit."

Afterwards, Lionel said: "I wish you'd taken me. Ernie Lotinga's just about my mark."

But they exchanged unrepentant glances. How could any lowbrow appreciate it with the subtlety of their enjoyment?

And all the time Eileen was perfectly right. Having been more than inoculated against Claudia three years ago, having had the disease and all its consequences, still Hugo was in no wise proof against her. Now that he was more of a man, now that he was forbidden fruit, now that the success of his novels was famous, she too felt more excited by him. Life had been so intellectually arid, she had missed him so. If only they could go on as they were now. She wanted no more from him, she was well content. But, alas he was in love with her again and knew it. Was it possible that he too would be content?

She couldn't smash up her home, Lionel's home, the home she herself had made. She couldn't leave Alan, her own little child, to be brought up by Lionel's mother or his second wife. Hugo couldn't ask it. Besides it would be too incongruous to run away with someone as young and innocent as he was. He wouldn't know what to do! It seemed better to have them both, Lionel and Hugo, try to make them both fairly, intermittently happy. Yet it was hardly ever right to try and have anything both ways. To take up lofty airs with Hugo now, to wash her hands of him and turn him, lonely, out of her life was unthinkable. And worst of all, worst of all, was to be a righteous woman taking all and giving nothing, a blameless woman keeping both lover and virtue, an immaculate woman preaching nobility and purity, allowing her cavalier neither mistress nor wife.

8

There is nothing in the conditions of life on this earth to make us think ourselves obliged to be good, to be sensitive, even polite; nor for the artist to feel himself compelled to begin a passage twenty times over again when the praise it evokes will matter little to the body devoured by worms. … All these obligations, which have no sanction in our present life, seem to belong to a different world, a world founded on goodness, on scruple, on sacrifice, a world … whence we come … perhaps to return there and live under the rule of the unknown laws which we have obeyed here … to which every deep intellectual labour draws us closer and which are invisible only—and not even!—to fools.

PROUST.

"We've got to go backwards or forwards. We can't stand still any more. You recognise that too, don't you, Claudia?"

"My dear, no. I can't think why we can't stay as we are. I don't know why a crisis should always have to occur. But this is ours."

It seemed to Claudia that they had been talking for hours, that Hugo had always been leaning against the mantelpiece, his smooth, coppery hair rumpled into a crest, his young face haggard and worn. It did not seem possible that she had only known for ten minutes that he wanted to leave her.

His voice went on, staccato with worry. And since on such occasions the tongue can only find its way to the same, well-worn hoard of clichés whether they be true from the heart or whether they be false, Hugo went on and on telling her that it was for her sake, for the sake of their ideals, because she was good, because he couldn't let her go through so much, and that the sacrifice was breaking him to pieces. She lifted her bowed, dark head and said a little wearily:

"Oh well, my darling! Isn't that what they always say?"

He made an entreating movement. His green eyes gazed at her as though in protest at a wanton blasphemy. She was ashamed that she could have said anything disagreeable. She seldom put obstacles in the chosen paths of her friends. She did not care to check their desires and their caprices. Therefore it was altogether against her principles to make it hard for anyone who really wanted, however mistakenly, to be good. She stretched out her hand impulsively to Hugo.

"I didn't mean to say anything hurting. I wouldn't ever think it was because you were tired. I'll never think like that about you. I'll always know you loved me."

"Loved you? You'll always know I love you still. For ever and ever, Claudia."

She turned her face away with a little doubting smile. Then she looked quickly back at him, fearing after all lest it were true. "Ah, no! Don't let me do that to you, Hugo."

They fell silent.

"I can't go," said Hugo suddenly. "I can't let you go and you not realising that it would be fifty times worse for me, that life would be utterly empty and finished without you. I thought you'd understand. But the way you looked just now. No, it's too much if you're going to think I'm tired."

She got up and went to him, laying her hand on his shoulder.

"Darling, I do understand. I do know how you feel. Lionel's such a good fellow. He's been so nice to us. Not only trusting us, but being so pleased, so innocent about us. You think that concealment might debase me or being thought evil harden me, and that either would be a wrong to my little child. You think that what might hurt others could bring us no true happiness. That the unlawful fulfilment of our love would desecrate something so beautiful and strong and holy that it needs no earthly fulfilment. That our love is worth it for what we've had, and the sacrifice worth it to keep our ideal."

His eyes lightened. He smiled almost radiantly, with great tenderness.

"You're wonderful, darling. I knew you'd understand. You feel the same way, don't you?"

"Of course I don't feel the same way!" said Claudia.

They sat down together on the sofa and he looked at her in bewilderment.

"How could you leave your child?"

"Should I have to do that?"

"Claudia!"

She told him: "I prefer French morality to American. We all agree it's better to keep your marriage vow. But if you can't, if another love upsets it, I think all that straightness-and-not-living-a-lie-and-being-true-to-yourself stuff, and throwing off the old responsibilities quick, is all selfish and wrong. I think you should still do everything to keep your home intact. Keep love and domesticity if need be in different boxes. I owe Lionel that much. I'm fond of him. I love Alan. It's—it's a dreadful thing, a man can't know how dreadful, to leave a child."

He looked unutterably shocked. "I thought you were brave. I thought you could face things. You'd want to have it both ways, live a lie and keep everything. How do you think that I could share you with Lionel?"

"I would leave my husband and my home and my child if you made me. At least, I don't know, I suppose I would."

"But you'd rather cheat."

She turned on him eagerly. "If I am unmoral, I was unmoral when

– 183 –

you fell in love with me. You knew me pretty well. Now you must love me, unmorality and all."

He cried: "I love you utterly. I love you altogether. Oh Claudia, I love you too much. I'll never let you go."

"Why can't we go on how we are, Hugo?"

"Claudia, you know I can't. I can't give you up either."

He knelt beside her and leant his head upon her breast. She gazed over him, stroking his hair. She had been thinking all the while that he was stronger than she. She had been waiting on his decision, and sure enough he had decided. He had gone heroically through the terrible task of breaking to her that she was to be abandoned. Now she suddenly realised that he was only stronger than she inasmuch as he was more good and no goodness can exist without strength. Fundamentally she was the stronger. After all, she was the better man of the two. She had got to help him because without her help he couldn't go. And beyond all question he wanted to.

She was in no hurry to break the respite of silence. She hugged his head to her, her fingers lightly brushing over his cheek. At last she said:

"Think gently of me, Hugo, but don't think of me too much. There's plenty of evil to remember of me, but if you must remember it, remember it in kindness; because I loved you or I would have shown you less. One is so uncovered, so defenceless in love."

He raised his face to hers and kissed her. They had never kissed before. She shut her eyes, longing for him to clasp her closely and kiss her as though he were her master and would not let her go. He kissed her and sighed and said hesitantly:

"What are we to do? Oh, darling, don't talk of my remembering evil! You've never been anything but an angel of goodness to me. You're the purest thing I've ever known."

She thought: "Your fault, or credit, not mine!"

She kissed him lightly on the forehead and gave him a little push towards the door.

"I shall live to be grateful to you for being so right, Hugo darling. You are right. And Lionel's a dear. I shall get along very well, really. We'll—get over it."

"I shall never get over it," said Hugo, his voice coming harsh and strained and uneven. He was worn out with trying to do right, and filled with an awful doubt as to whether Lionel's trust, Claudia's sanctity, their child's background and his own conception of love, yes and a whole world of ideals, could be worth this shattering sacrifice. But after one last, sacramental, long embrace he wrenched himself away and went laggingly through the door.

In the forefront of Claudia's mind was the thought that she mustn't cry. Because she felt that she could cry for ever. Dreadful so to lose control. Degrading to cry for a man. Un-self-respecting, almost unclean to blot out one's beauty with a hideous morass of tears. Dry-eyed, she went over to the panatrope and switched on the electric current. There was a record already there. She put the needle in place, and set it going. The thing had a sort of mesmeric swing to it. Its rhythm made a weird background to her chaos of thoughts. Like the quick, cynical accompaniment of Don Giovanni's languishing serenade. Every time the end of the record was reached she put the needle back to the beginning and ran it through over again, lest without that hypnotic clamour she should think too clearly.

> Then take your last look upon sunshine and brook,
> And send your regrets to the Czar,
> By which I imply ...

So she would never see Hugo again. Never, never. Not any more. She had been mad to be so scrupulous, so generous, so considerate. She needn't have let him go. You thought about other people when they were there, and when you were left alone with only yourself to think of you wished you had done more of that when thoughts could be of any avail.

> Oh stranger when passing, ah pray for the soul
> Of Abdul Abulbul Amir.

> A Muscovite maiden her lone vigil keeps
> By the light of the pale polar star,
> And the name that she murmurs so oft as she weeps …

She hoped that he would nearly forget her. That was as much as she could honestly rise to. He must have been much better than she was, or else a poor fish, to end it so.

> And send your regrets to the Czar.
> By which I imply you are going to die,
> Count Ivan Skivinsky Skivar!

He wouldn't telephone. He wouldn't write. He was strong enough for that—now that she had let him go. She must think about Lionel, about little Alan, about running the house. Oh, any of the machinery of life. She wanted a new dress.

> … bravest by far in the ranks of the Shah
> Was Abdul …

A good one. Something that looked really dressed, or undressed. She'd never lose her figure if she could help it.

> … was a man by the name
> Of Ivan Skivinsk …

Lionel liked kedgeree. She must remember to order it for him. It hadn't turned up for ages.

> Then take your last look upon sunshine and brook,
> And send your regrets …

Men always forgot and women never did. Everyone knew that. Oh God!

> Czar Petrovitch too in his spectacles blue …

She had probably been quite, quite wrong. She had wanted Hugo to be happy. Now surely she had made him miserable. He was all alone. He would be so terribly lonely. Ah, but he had wanted to go.

> By the light of the pale polar star,
> And the name that she murmurs so oft as she weeps
> Is Ivan Skivinsky Skivar.

At length she forgot to put the needle back to the beginning of the record. In silence the current flowed on waiting to be switched off. Claudia was having her long-denied cry at last.

Lionel found her so, coming in shortly after, when she lay all storm shaken among the sofa cushions. He was surprised, but not very much surprised. It was a long time since Claudia had cried, still women were like that, poor little dears. It was even rather jolly to find them all so much alike.

"Clau darling! This is like the dear old honeymoon! What's the matter?" A sudden ghastly thought struck him. "Nothing wrong with young Alan?"

"Nothing's the matter," wailed Claudia. This was exactly what Lionel had supposed.

She raised her weary face, all ugly and marred with crying, and held out her arms to him. She was scarcely crying for Hugo now; she had cried for so long that she just couldn't stop. Lionel held her tightly to him and they huddled together among the sofa cushions, her face pressed in the crook of his neck and shoulder, her sobs gradually subsiding into gasping, irregular, painful breaths.

"There, there, Clau, you old ass! My darling sweet," said Lionel. He was thoroughly enjoying himself.

She began to explain. "Cook's given notice and Alan's been in a temper and I've had a beastly letter from Eileen and I look like hell in my new hat."

"You'd look like hell in anything or nothing now, darling. But I expect you'll look all right in it when you've washed your face."

Clinging to him, feeling a little better, she breathed automatically the age-old formula, "Oh God! I wish I were dead."

"Of course you do!" said Lionel cheerfully, and slapped her on the back.

9

←→

The strand of the daughters of the sunset,
The apple-tree, the singing and the gold.

                    GILBERT MURRAY's *Hyppolitus*.

Ashurst rose, took his wife's sketch, and stared at it in silence.
"Is the foreground right, Frank?"
"Yes."
"But there's something wanting, isn't there?"
Ashurst nodded. Wanting? The apple-tree, the singing and the gold!

                    The Apple-Tree, GALSWORTHY.

Claudia never ceased to be amazed, when she thought of it, at the speed with which she got over Hugo. At first she was rather proud of her own powers of recuperation. For at first it wasn't easy. It was a dreadful sentimental wrench. But as it rapidly did become perfectly easy, her powers of recuperation almost alarmed her. Considering the possible courses she had contemplated she really should have been heartbroken for quite a little while. Again, it seemed far worse to have hurt Hugo if his hurt was out of all proportion to her own. Altogether it was a little officious of Time the Great Healer to heal at quite such a rate.

Had she just used Hugo as something to let off steam at, and, now that he had served his useful end, could she return unmarked, unaltered, to take up again the way from which she had swerved? It seemed so cold-blooded, and yet she wasn't cold-blooded. Light, then, light. Had she loved him? Or had she just been affectionate and responsive? Had she never loved him? Was he just a farewell fling to the abstract love of her dreaming, to the moon that she must want in vain till she ceased to want so unpractical, cumbersome a thing? Just a proof to satisfy her that a tract of her secret country must for ever lie fallow? Or was it that Lionel's brawn weighed heavier in the scales than brain, that intellect was too cool a thing, soul too remote a thing, to carry her away, that in her heart she must still worship breadth of shoulder and accuracy of eye?

It was all very, very disturbing. And yet it couldn't be wrong not to brood over an unlawful love. It must be right to be content with your husband and child and the allotted life you led.

The Byngs had their domesticated side. They were both devoted to Alan who showed signs of being a pleasant mixture of the two, favouring his father's looks and his mother's quickness. They often liked a peaceful evening, reading to each other or sticking photographs of and paragraphs about their activities into an album. But they were well and truly in the social whirl and they loved it. A continual round of the same faces, the same haunts, the same standard of flirtation and dress, the same jokes and almost the same shows, produced a soothing, hypnotic effect of perpetual motion, equally avoiding effort and stagnation. As long as wheels of some sort do go round, let us by all means run for ever in the same circle.

They were very proud of each other. He admired her social success, the increasing sophistication of her looks. But he did love her for her good temper, her kindness, her generosity, her sense of fun, and his private conception of something sweet and essentially Claudia. And in much the same way she really was fond of him for his good temper, his kindness, his generosity, his good-mixing, and her own private conception of something rather sweet and Lionel. And though he might not be sparkling like Alan Vane, or responsive like Guy Verney, or clever and high-minded like Hugo, still he was very, very much handsomer! What abiding satisfactions were his magnificent looks, his physique, his wonderful, disappointing eyes!

Claudia then felt thoroughly happy one March afternoon, as she and young Alan motored to the Heseltine flat to have tea with Daddy. Daddy had stayed up an extra day on purpose, for it was the only day that week that his daughter and his grandson could both manage. So it was altogether quite an occasion. She might even tell her father—but no, that piece of news could be told better the week-end after next when she and Lionel would spend three nights at Chesnor, and Mother could hear it too. Sylvia was a pretty name for a girl, but she would be fairly gravelled by another boy.

Alan was in great form. He held her hand tightly in his sticky one— sticky and dirty again already, how did they do it, bless them?—and talked all the way. His conversation was not as yet very connected, but it demanded much attention just the same. It was jolly that for a few more years she could kiss his dark curls and his soft, soft face without his thinking her effeminate. But looking ahead was jolly too. Alan's first pony. Lionel proudly teaching him to ride. ...

Alan and his grandfather were great friends, and after tea they retired together to have a treasure hunt in the latter's bedroom. Claudia sat on in the drawing-room window seat in a mood of idle speculation.

Vaguely, her father often reminded her a little of Hugo. He, and her mother too, were more in his line of country than in hers and Lionel's. And yet she couldn't see much wrong with herself and Lionel. They weren't blind to the responsibility of their good fortune. They were generous both in hospitality and in charity. They were "very good sorts." Why should he work if he needn't, and didn't want to? What could he work at? On the whole, Lionel lived up to his own lights on living. Could she say the same of herself?

Claudia was not given to introspection. Generally she was almost too easy going and unmorbid. But it was, she felt, one thing to know what was wrong and comfortably to ignore it, cheerfully forget it, and quite another to lose the capacity for realising that there was anything wrong at all. She was and would be content, but as a matter of academic interest, as a mental and spiritual exercise, she must be able to put her finger on what was amiss.

It wasn't really that she never thought of Hugo and Eileen, and never missed them at all. She thought of them from time to time with love, but she was so personal that since they had left her life, all that they had stood for had gone out of it too. Could she be so adaptable that having no one now with whom to share soul experiences she simply ceased to have them?

Dash it all, what was wrong with her? She was a person anyone could tell their troubles or trust their secrets to. And surely it must be right to be contented. With Alan's crowing laugh coming through the wall, it *must* be right to be contented. Wasn't happiness after all the test, the proof, of good heart and good sense as well as good digestion? Nothing was commoner than depression and discontent. Those were bad things and quite too easy. Besides, they befell the Cazlitts and the Joyces, while Reynoldses and Heseltines were happy. Well then? "No, I remember the answer," she told herself, and getting up she found a volume of Aldous Huxley and turned the leaves till she found a certain paragraph. She read:

"Nemesis isn't a policewoman. Nemesis isn't moral. At least she is only incidentally moral, more or less by accident. Nemesis is something like gravitation, indifferent. All that she does is to ensure that you shall reap what you sow. And if you sow self-stultification … you reap grotesque humiliation. But if you're already reduced by your offences to a subhuman condition, you won't notice that the grotesque humiliation is a humiliation. That's your explanation why Nemesis sometimes seems to reward. What she brings is a humiliation only in the absolute sense—for the ideal and complete human being; or at any rate, in practice, for the nearly complete, the approaching-the-ideal human being. For the subhuman specimen it may seem a triumph, a consummation, a fulfilment of the heart's desire."

Claudia was pleased with her cleverness—though it was really Mr. Huxley's—in disposing of her own case. She felt quite happy; happy, as she generally was; happy as she now understood happiness. The sun came out in splendid generosity, flooding over the jars of white and mauve lilac from Chesnor and, which was more to the point, illuming the little ruby ring that Lionel had given her a few days ago for her twenty-eighth birthday. Not that she didn't care for lilac too: indeed she and Lionel were both very fond of it. And as the sun came, golden and comforting, a barrel organ began to play the "Blue Danube" outside.

"Why worry?" thought Claudia. "It's all a toss up. One can't help oneself. With me it was just a matter of which of three week-ends I chanced to choose five years ago. If I had gone to Hugo's, or to Lalage's for that matter, he and I would have married, and life would have been one lovely adventure for both of us all in the heights of virtue and pure thought. I might have met an unknown affinity at Lalage's and made earth heaven. Well it's no good cursing one's luck, but they can't blame me."

And she asked herself, did it matter that now the countries she had vainly imagined she might penetrate with Hugo must for her remain for ever unexplored? She said, as a solid, practical *amende honorable* to the Holy Ghost:

"As we've got so much money and a happy home, perhaps it's our duty to have a child every other year."

PART VI

PART VI

WHICH WAY?

Room, while I stand outside you in the gloom,
Your tranquil-toned interior, void of me,
Seems part of my own self which I can see.
...
Light, while I stand outside you in the night,
Shutting the door on what has housed so much,
Nor hand, nor eye, nor intellect could touch,—
Cell to whose firelit walls I say farewell,
Could I condense five winters in one thought,
Then might I know my unknown self and tell
What our confederate silences have wrought.

SIEGFRIED SASSOON.

There was no one in the room. Blinds and curtains were closed; the light of the skies, if any, was shut out. There was about the place the curious, expectant air of a stage set for the curtain to rise. For while hill and plain and valley are eternal and care not what fugitive dramas take them for setting, a room exists only for men and women. It is there to hear their many lies and their frightened truths; to shelter their secret thoughts; to look on at their moods of helpless revolt—things can never be the same again ... I must do something! ... I must do something! ... And there is nothing to do but have a bath and go to bed. An empty room is always waiting.

There was a fire in the room; very comforting and gay. It threw a lovely liquid sheet of orange on the big armchairs each side of it. It sent a flickering glow on to the gallery table where lay weekly and daily papers, magazines, a few books lately thrown down. In front of the fire was a low stool, behind that a deep, soft sofa. Against one wall were shelves of books; opposite, a writing-table framed by the dull, peach-coloured curtains of the windows. Branches and trails of flowers stood in great jars, drained of their colour in the shadows but not of their faint sweetness. The cushions were fluffed out, inviting. An antique clock marked time in a hushed monotone. Only the fire was alive, consuming its life—for what? Then the door opened and as Claudia came with hurried steps into the fire's glow, two open letters in her hand, the telephone began ringing. She shut the door and turned up the lights.

AFTERWORD

In the past two decades or so, the term 'sliding doors moment' has been used to describe how seemingly inconsequential instances can greatly alter the course of one's life, or even of history. The term refers to Peter Howitt's 1998 film *Sliding Doors*, which follows two parallel timelines. In one Gwyneth Paltrow's Helen catches the London Underground train she is running for; while in the other she misses it. One of these leads to catching her boyfriend having sex with another woman; the other does not. Similar to the butterfly effect, a tiny incident causes ripples with much further reaching consequences – and the film plays out the parallel timelines simultaneously.

This central conceit has been linked to J.B. Priestley's 1932 play *Dangerous Corner*, in which a chance remark by one of the characters leads to the exposure of affairs and other secrets, and even to suicide. The final scene of the play shows what would have happened if the remark had not been made – leaving a happily-ever-after for all the characters. Only a year earlier, Theodora Benson's fourth novel, *Which Way?*, explored the same idea.

Appropriately for a comparison with Priestley, the opening section that establishes 'the four cross roads' feels very much like the setting up of a play. The novel's first words, 'There was no one in the room. Blinds and curtains were closed', are like stage directions, and this continues in a description of the fireplace, the book-laden table, the sofa. And then …

> The door opened and as Claudia came with hurried steps into the fire's glow, two open letters in her hand, the telephone began ringing. She shut the door and turned up the lights.

The lights are up and the play is ready to begin. The letters and the telephone call are offering her invitations for an upcoming weekend – and her 'sliding doors moment' is choosing which to accept. The course of Claudia's life will take very different turns, depending on her decision. Ultimately, two lead to marriage and all three lead to romantic unfaithfulness of one sort or another, and her state of mind at the end of each section varies significantly. More than this, though, each path shows Claudia choosing a different way to be a woman in the 1930s.

Before Claudia reaches the crossroads, she muses on her romantic future with her friend Eileen. Together, they sing the refrain from a nineteenth-century folk song, 'I Know Where I'm Going': "I know where I'm going / and I know who's going with me / And I know who I love / but the de'il knows who I'll marry!" The ballad is about a wealthy young woman who has fallen for Johnny, a man with a bad reputation – like the woman, Claudia doesn't know whom she'll marry, though Johnny stand-ins may appear later.

The initial choice between the three paths seems to be between three men: glamorous, married Guy; dependable novelist Hugo; Adonis-but-dim Lionel. But though each invitation does lead to Claudia developing a relationship with these respective men, it is the shifts in Claudia that stand out the most. While recognisably the same person we've been introduced to in the opening quarter of the novel, different facets of her character come to the fore.

By 'turning to the left' and accepting the invitation to stay with Lalage and encounter Guy again, 'an ordinary enough man of thirty-seven', it isn't long before she is having an affair with him. There is background discussion of a divorce trial, echoing their affair, though ultimately there is no real likelihood that Guy will follow suit. There were only 3,764 divorces in 1931 – a number that wouldn't significantly jump until the Second World War. Claudia has fallen into becoming 'the other woman', as lightly and wittily as she does anything else, and it means that, when their relationship suddenly ends, there is no obligatory drawn-out conclusion.

The end is not on her own terms. Turning to the left has handed most of the power to Guy – even in one of their first meetings, he 'took her arm in a firm grip and steered her briskly to the house', dictating her actions while she falls in step with him. So, while she 'protracted the death agonies of the relationship', as Benson drily phrases it, Guy makes 'polite, convincing, regretful excuses' to all her suggestions for meeting. Claudia believes that she has become an example of a type she despises: 'difficult women who want to be exacting and make themselves felt instead of being natural.'

The section ends with her doctrine being that she can only find happiness by reconciling two apparent opposites; 'to be free and not to be lonely'. The narrator quickly rules out two possible stereotypes for Claudia's future – she will go neither 'to the good' or 'to the bad'; the former being good works like 'slum visiting', and the latter not explicitly spelled out. It is the only path of the three that leads to happiness, even though she thinks she has missed

> ... the sweetest of men to love and be loved by always, an interesting, intellectual life, a house of my own, children to beguile and worry and fill my middle age, perfect happiness—if

I hadn't just happened to go to Farling instead of Gloucestershire for a week-end five years ago.

'Going straight on' looks at what happens if she had gone to Farling – and, of course, it is not the idyllic vision that she imagines. She enters marriage with a sense of obligation, and without fully knowing everything it is likely to entail: she avoids hearing 'various things of vaguely sinister import' from her mother, though this level of ignorance was far less common by the late 1920s (when the scene is set) than it had been a decade earlier. Marie Stopes' 1918 work *Married Love* was the most popular of the many books that explained sex and sexuality to a generation of women – supposedly aimed at married women, as the title suggests, but doubtless read by many others. *Married Love* had sold 750,000 copies by the time *Which Way?* was published and spawned a number of imitations. Other guides relating to the infertility issues faced by the couple would also have been available, though with little practicable advice to give other than hoping for the best.

If she was the 'other woman' in the first section, she becomes an adulterous wife in the second – again with Guy. Both sections end with some regret at the choice of invitations she made. Here she tells Guy, "If I'd chosen a different week-end visit five years ago, you and I would have been perfectly safe and happy for evermore." Benson lets the sentence hang heavy with irony; we already know, of course, that this wouldn't have been the case. But this is no moral tale. It isn't unfaithfulness that leads to unhappiness – the two may coincide, but without causation. Wider society, in each section of *Which Way?*, seems equally unfazed by Claudia's closeness to a man she isn't married to. In the 1930s, as in many decades, these moral censorships struck more keenly at women from lower classes. While a maid might lose her job for having 'followers', a 'higher-class' woman of the period could conceivably be viewed simply as bohemian for similar behaviour – as long as nothing sexual was too overt.

The final pathway, to the right, leads Claudia to the opposite of Hugo: Lionel is an 'astonishingly handsome' polo player and not at all intelligent or cultured. With him, she quickly becomes the type of 1930s woman whose defence against the ego of an unintelligent man is to quash signs of her own intelligence. She cannot be blamed for the standards of her age, of course; in her early conversations with Lionel, she tells him that a female friend is 'not very' clever – an assurance given 'loyally', and clearly considered to the friend's credit. He openly tells Claudia that he wouldn't love her as much if she weren't pretty.

The person that Claudia becomes with Hugo and Lionel respectively is subtly shown through the ways that these sections use quotations in the characters' speech and thought. While the narrative with Lionel often reverts to popular dance-hall music of the period, such as 'Abdul Abulbul Amir', Hugo and Claudia covertly quote the Bible to each other. Claudia asks, "How shall they hear without a preacher?", with reference to Romans 10:14, which exhorts believers to share the good news of Jesus. A couple of pages later Hugo follows suit, when he questions whether he would be willing to "drink of the cup you drank of", obliquely citing Matthew 20:22, where Jesus rhetorically asks two of His disciples if they would be willing to suffer as He must suffer. Hugo reads her Shakespeare (*The Tempest* and *Cymbeline* are quoted) as well as more recent poems by Edna St Vincent Millay and Alfred Noyes. Their shared cultural touchstones are far more elevated.

Indeed, when Claudia first meets Hugo and he introduces himself as the novelist of *Paid in Full*, *The House of the Fool*, and

Celia Remembered, she rattles off a list of titles he might have written – *The Good Companions*, *Portrait in a Mirror*, *Brief Candles*, and *The Edwardians*. These books, by J.B. Priestley, Charles Morgan, Aldous Huxley, and Vita Sackville-West respectively, were all published in the couple of years before *Which Way?*. Both Hugo and the reader are expected to recognise references to recent literary culture, as well as scorning the popular novelists Dornford Yates and E. Phillips Oppenheim as the reading material of a "half-baked nitwit".

Conversely, when Lionel does read to a pregnant Claudia, 'badly but not unintelligibly', he chooses 'rousing classics of schoolroom, and the Book Society's novels'. Set up in 1929 with a selection committee including Hugh Walpole and J.B. Priestly, the Book Society was a 'book-of-the-month' club which sent subscribers a book and a selection of recommended alternatives if they didn't want it. Though selections included authors such as Virginia Woolf and D.H. Lawrence, domestic and 'middlebrow' fiction were the mainstay and the Society and others like it were frequently disparaged by highbrow authors and critics as commodifying literature and dictating that people should enjoy a mediocre literary diet.

But Claudia is not satisfied with either Hugo or Lionel. It is partly as an escape from Hugo's intellectualism that Claudia starts to see Guy. One of their outings is to Nervo and Knox – Jimmy Nervo and Teddy Knox – a music-hall double act who combined circus acts with humorous songs and physical comedy. They appeared on stage and screen and, in the year *Which Way?* was published, were founding members of the popular comedy group the Crazy Gang.

Guy and Claudia return, quoting parts of the act – 'Cut yourself a piece of throat', for instance, which appears to be a riff on a popular 1920s tune 'Cut Yourself a Piece of Cake' – and other stray lines that suggest Benson may well have attended this or a similar show herself.

They agreed how heavenly it was to be low-brow, how useless it
would have been to have gone to this perfect slapstick performance
with Hugo. [...] Guy and Claudia exchanged unrepentant glances.
He'd have been precious, patronisingly intellectual. He wouldn't
have enjoyed in the right way.

The trend of enjoying 'bad' entertainment ironically is clearly not new,
and it is something Claudia wishes to resist. But in the final section,
where she is married to 'straightforward, stupid' Lionel, she goes with
Hugo to see Ernest Lotinga, a comic actor known for his character
'Jimmy Josser', using a contemporary slang term for an unintelligent
person. They love it. She suggests Noel Coward's 1930 *Private Lives*
"would be a complete flop here" – it was, at that time, a recent play
and remains popular to this day, about a divorced couple who find
they are honeymooning with their new spouses in adjacent hotel
rooms. The comedy of mismatched couples repeating their mistakes
might ring true with readers of *Which Way?*.

In one of the cleverest moments of reversal in the novel, when
Lionel says he wishes he'd seen Lotinga with them, Hugo and
Claudia 'exchange unrepentant glances. How could any lowbrow
appreciate it with the subtlety of their enjoyment?' The glances remain
unrepentant, but the person receiving Claudia's glance has changed
– and so has its purport. No longer is Claudia defending the lowbrow
against the intellectual; rather, she is defending it *for* the intellectual.

It's a small moment that sums up Claudia's personality in the
novel: a flexible one, ready to be moulded by her surroundings and the
people she knows. When Hugo is explaining the theme of his novel to
Claudia, he describes a woman "who's got to face her crisis. Shall she
leave her husband or not?". Ultimately, he says, she will not because
"she's not the type [...] She has to go through this hell of mental strife,

and any passing acquaintance could tell the outcome long before with hardly a thought". *Which Way?* ultimately disputes this reasoning. Claudia is the same woman, whichever pathway she chooses, but whether she becomes a wife, a mistress, a dutiful mother is little to do with her 'type'. Even the core of her morality shifts. Her interests, the way she presents herself, and the things that make her happy are all malleable – so, when Claudia is choosing between three invitations, she is ultimately choosing between three selves. The only consistency is 'Blue Danube' played in the background. Benson uses a sort of 'multiverse' to show the instability of the self – exploring very different positions within the parameters available to women in the 1930s.

Simon Thomas

Series consultant **Simon Thomas** created the middlebrow blog Stuck in a Book in 2007. He is also the co-host of the popular podcast Tea or Books? Simon has a PhD from Oxford University in Interwar Literature.

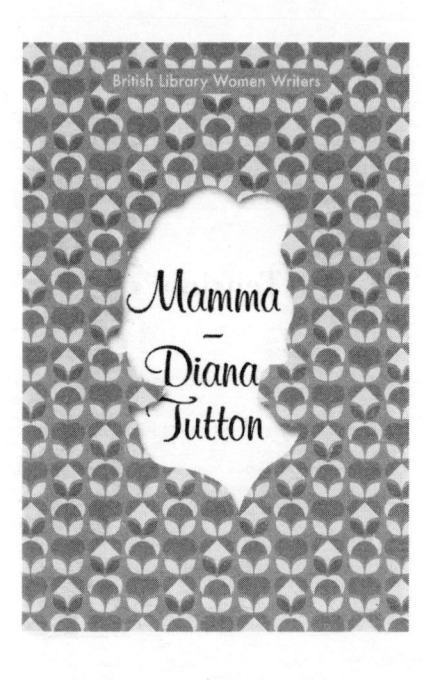

Joanna sat with her cheek against her [Libby's] shining hair. She had hardly thought of Steven since he slammed his way out of the house, but now, welling up within her and pouring out over her love for Libby, came an intolerable flood of envy.

Widowed at 21 with a young baby, Joanna Malling finds her solitary existence upended twenty years later when her daughter Libby moves in with her new husband. At 35, Steven is closer in age to Joanna than Libby. What begins as an awkward relationship between mother and son-in-law evolves into something more intimate and Joanna must wrestle with re-awakened emotions and the conflict between desire and loyalty.

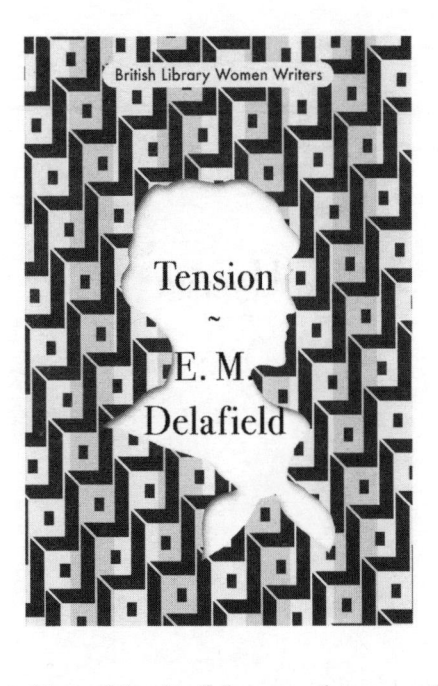

"I know that things of that kind always are known, and the people I've been thrown with, sooner or later, always turned out to have heard the story. Or if they hadn't," said Miss Marchrose in a voice of calm despair, "someone took the trouble to tell them."

Miss Marchrose is about to discover that she cannot escape her past when she takes up a new position at a secretarial college in the south west of England. Following insinuations dropped by the director's wife, she becomes the subject of a whispering campaign which threatens her professional career and personal happiness.

ALSO AVAILABLE

"I want to stay just as we are for ever and ever. Just like this;
you and me and the moor, and nobody else."

Ruan Ashley looks back on her childhood in a coming-of-age novel
set before the First World War. Ruan is an intelligent and imaginative
child, who gradually comes to understand the nuances of the adult
world around her as she moves from the Manse, under the strict rule
of her father, to Cobbetts, her mother's ancestral home, and back to
the moor above the town where she was born. Her life is shaped by
tragedy, but also the warmth of enduring friendships, particularly
with David, who shares her love of the wild expanse and colours of
the moor.

*"Don't marry a woman with a past. Her past will be
her own present and your future."*

Sally Lunton is on the rocks and in search of a husband. As the First
World War grips Europe, she flees Paris to the safety of village life in
Little Crampton under the roof of her guardian, The Revd Lovelady.

Sally is a warm-hearted, spirited heroine, who is determined to settle
into a comfortable life now she is in her early thirties. But she has a
rival for the affections of the village's most eligible bachelor, and her
pursuit is further frustrated by a soldier tortured by his experience at
the Front, and a secret in her bohemian past which follows her home.

British Library Women Writers

Tea Is So Intoxicating

Mary Essex

"I shall turn this into a tea-house, with lunches if requested, and shall serve pleasant meals in the orchard," announced David, "and with my penchant for cooking I ought to make a fortune."
"O dear!" said Germayne.

The prospect of a new tea garden opening in the village causes great consternation. With rumour rife that David and Germayne are not 'properly married', the lady of the manor makes it her mission to shut the enterprise down. With Germayne at her wits' end, the situation is further complicated by the arrival, first of Mimi the cake cook, and then her daughter Ducks followed by her first husband Digby.